"Whoever attacked me at the park still wants me dead," Julie said.

She spoke with such certainty and calm, yet every muscle in Zach's body tensed, every hair on the back of his neck stood on end. She was in danger.

He swallowed the guilt that rose in his throat. "I am sorry. This is my fault." Every syllable threatened to choke him, each one harder than the last. "I promised I'd take care of you. And instead I revealed right where you are."

She shook her head and slipped her hand into his and squeezed. "It wasn't your fault, Zach. But he'll come looking for me again."

The fingers in his grip bega̶̶̶̶̶̶̶̶ even more with every rise ̶̶̶̶̶̶̶̶ terrified.

Whoever they were dealing with, whoever had attacked her in that park, had disappeared.

* * *

WITNESS PROTECTION: Hiding in plain sight

Books by Liz Johnson

Love Inspired Suspense

The Kidnapping of Kenzie Thorn
Vanishing Act
Code of Justice
*A Promise to Protect
*SEAL Under Siege
Stolen Memories

*Men of Valor

LIZ JOHNSON

After graduating from Northern Arizona University in Flagstaff with a degree in public relations, Liz Johnson set out to work in the Christian publishing industry, which was her lifelong dream. In 2006 she got her wish when she accepted a publicity position with a major trade book publisher. While working as a publicist in the industry, she decided to pursue her other dream—becoming an author. Along the way to having her novels published, she wrote articles for several magazines and worked as a freelance editorial consultant.

Liz makes her home in Nashville, Tennessee, where she enjoys theater, exploring her new home and making frequent trips to Arizona to dote on her nephew and three nieces. She loves stories of true love with happy endings.

STOLEN MEMORIES
LIZ JOHNSON

HARLEQUIN® LOVE INSPIRED® SUSPENSE

Special thanks and acknowledgment are given to Liz Johnson for her contribution to the Witness Protection miniseries.

Recycling programs
for this product may
not exist in your area.

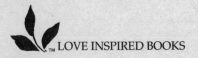

™ LOVE INSPIRED BOOKS

ISBN-13: 978-0-373-44586-8

STOLEN MEMORIES

www.Harlequin.com

Printed in U.S.A.

This is the covenant I will make with them
after that time, says the Lord.
I will put my laws in their hearts,
and I will write them on their minds.
—*Hebrews* 10:16

For Kaye and Ruth, who encouraged me
as I wrote this book. True friendship is an
uncommon and special gift. I'll never forget yours.

ONE

Zach Jones ran his hand down his face until his fingers covered a yawn. Letting out a muted sigh, he stared through the windshield of his parked car, seeing nothing but the lights lining the Minneapolis street. After a long day of chasing down dead ends, he was ready for a couple days off.

A quick glance at the clock on his dashboard revealed that his shift was almost over. Time to head back to the station before turning in for the night. He'd just put the unmarked sedan into gear when the police radio in his car squawked, and he leaned over to turn it up.

"Possible dead body at the corner of Thomas Road and Gavel Drive at Webster Park." His stomach lurched, his pulse flying. That was just a few blocks away.

Tossing the radio handset into the empty passenger seat, he flipped on the sirens and pulled onto the nearly deserted road. Usually he was the last one to the scene. Homicide was always called in after a dozen patrol officers had swarmed the area.

This close to the scene, he'd probably even beat the uniforms there.

"This is Jones. I'm en route."

The dispatcher replied with a quick, "Ten-four." Then

after a short pause she added, "Two boys cutting through the park found the body."

"Are they still at the scene?"

"Yes."

"Good. Tell them to stay away from the body but not to move. I'll have questions for them later."

Trees just beginning to sprout their spring leaves sailed by as he maneuvered around a car pulled over to the side of the road to get out of his way. The lights of the restaurants and stores of the commercial district to his left faded, his mind focused on the scene he was about to reach.

Pulling off the road, he parked at the entrance of a walking path, turned off the sirens but left the red-and-blue lights flashing. He was the first on the scene. He slipped his phone into his pocket, tucked his flashlight into his belt and pulled on rubber gloves as he followed the beam of his headlights.

Two boys, probably no more than twelve, sat next to each other on a wooden bench, hugging their hockey skates as though he was going to demand they give them up. He pushed back his jacket to show them the badge hanging around his neck, a late winter wind seeping through the fabric of his shirt. "You boys call the cops?"

The bigger boy nodded a mop of dark brown hair and let go of his skates long enough to point behind him into the shadows.

Zach squinted but couldn't make out a form between the tree trunks. "Did you go near the body?"

"No, sir." Again from the bigger boy. The little one with the blond crew cut hadn't blinked since Zach arrived. He was probably in shock from what he'd seen.

How bad was it over there?

His skin crawled, the hair on his arms standing up. It

wasn't from the cold. Or even from this case. This wasn't his first day in the department.

It was something in the air. Something that, after ten years with the Minneapolis P.D., he could almost smell. Something that, after all this time, he still couldn't name.

"You boys stay here. Okay? Other officers are on their way. And I'll be right back."

Swinging his flashlight across the grass at his feet to make sure he didn't inadvertently step on a vital piece of evidence, he picked his way in the direction the kid had first indicated. After thirty yards, the light from his car was almost no help. A curtain of rich gray clouds had fallen in front of the moon, so he slowed to a near crawl.

And then he saw it.

A crimson pool coated a patch of lawn the size of a dinner plate.

Shivers ran down his spine and he sucked in a quick breath as he flicked his light up to illuminate the body. It was a woman with long dark hair, which was matted across half of her face with her own blood. She lay on her side, one arm stretched out under her head and the other curled under her chin. Her full lips were nearly white.

His stomach clenched.

This part never got easier.

Without a doubt this was going to be the worst night of someone's life. That person was going to get a call that would change everything, that would shatter a heart.

But Zach would do everything he could to make sure that the person responsible never had the opportunity to do this again, to destroy a family again.

Stepping around the stain of evidence, he reached her side and squatted next to her. The part of her face that he could still make out was covered with scratches and already turning purple. A gash above her left eye disappeared into her hairline and looked to be the source of the bloodstain he'd dodged. Someone had beaten the tar out of her.

A drop slipped down her forehead, and he paused.

Dead bodies in a position like this didn't usually keep bleeding.

He snapped his gloves at the wrists to make sure they were on tight and pressed two fingers against the spot where her left palm met her forearm. Holding his breath, he waited.

There, beneath the skin and barely palpable, was a pulse.

His heartbeat jackhammered just below his throat.

"Ma'am. Ma'am, can you hear me?"

No response.

He grabbed his phone and punched in the number for the dispatcher. He didn't even wait for an answer. As soon as the line was picked up, he said, "This is Detective Jones." He spit out his badge number, standing and searching the streets for any sign of the ambulance that wasn't going to be in enough of a hurry to get there. "I'm at Webster Park, and the possible homicide victim is not DOA. Repeat, the victim is alive. I need an ambulance and backup here ASAP."

His voice shook a little on the last word, and he took a steadying breath. He didn't have live victims. He'd only seen one other in the three years since making detective and joining Homicide.

This one was about as close to death, but still breathing, as he'd ever seen.

"Ten-four. Paramedics are en route."

"ETA?"

"Three minutes."

He dropped back by her side, keeping his finger pressed against her wrist. The steady thumps under his touch kept his hope alive, but only just.

Lord, please let this one live.

He didn't have an explanation for the intensity of the longing in his heart, but he knew she didn't deserve to die like this, alone and abandoned in a city park that hadn't seen much traffic since the city started massive construction on a walking bridge.

Someone didn't want her quickly found or able to tell her tale.

Sirens carried through the trees, ringing between buildings as they drew nearer. The band around his heart loosened.

"Don't worry. Help is on its way."

Her only response was the steady beat at his fingertips.

"Hang in there. You just have to hang in there a little while longer. Then we'll find whoever did this, and he'll pay. I promise."

Everything before that moment was blank.

It took considerable effort, but she pried her right eye open far enough to cringe at the glaring light wedged between white ceiling tiles. Pain like a knife sliced at her temple. She tried to lift her hand to press it to her skull. Maybe that would keep it from shattering. But her arm had tripled in size and weighed more than the rest of her body. She could only lift it an inch from where it lay at her side.

Fire shot from her elbow to the tip of her middle finger, a sob escaping from somewhere deep in her chest and leaving a scar inside her throat as it escaped.

"Julie?"

Julie? She turned to look in the direction of the voice to see who else was in the room, but something plastic tugged against her nose. An oxygen cannula. She didn't even try to lift her hand to adjust it, instead rolling her eye as far as she could.

A gentle hand with cold fingers pressed against her forearm, but the face was just out of reach. "Julie? How are you feeling?"

Who was Julie? There wasn't anyone else in her limited line of sight, but that didn't mean the other girl wasn't close by.

A face—round and blurry—appeared right above her. Wide-set blue eyes shone with compassion and the same brilliance as her white smile. "I'm Tammy, your ICU nurse." Cool fingers secured the tubing back into place and brushed across her forehead. "You've been here quite a while. I'm glad you decided to wake up on my shift, Julie." A low chuckle followed. "Oh dear, I've gotten so used to calling you that. I'll have to stop."

What was she doing in the ICU? On a hospital bed in the ICU? And why had the nurse been calling her Julie?

That wasn't her name.

"I know someone who's been looking forward to talking with you."

She blinked and tried to ask who, but her voice cracked. Only a croak escaped before Tammy pressed a straw to her lips. "Drink a little bit of this."

She did as the nurse instructed, the tepid water like a creek in the Sahara, soothing her throat as she swallowed it but leaving most of the area untouched. She tried for a longer sip and more water but choked on it. Tammy pulled the cup away and patted a tissue where a trickle had escaped down her chin.

She jolted at the touch, pain searing to the bone.

"I'm sorry. Your stitches are probably still a bit tender. But you're healing nicely."

Healing? How long had she been in the unit? How had she gotten there? Because she'd just been—

"If you're ready, I'm going to let Detective Jones know

that he can come in and see you. He's been waiting to talk with you for three days."

She tried to shake her head. A detective? As in a police officer? Why were the police coming to see her? What had she done?

She didn't want to see anyone, let alone a detective. But Tammy disappeared before she could get her body to respond. Everything was moving slower than it should. Her muscles, her joints, her brain.

Only the low hum of Tammy's voice carried across the room. "Now remember, she hasn't even seen the doctor yet. Don't give her a hard time."

A deep voice agreed that he'd try not to.

As if to show off just how slow her mind was moving, Tammy reappeared almost the instant that the conversation ended, one hand resting on an arm that belonged to someone just outside her range of vision. "This is Detective Jones. He's with the Minneapolis P.D. I'll let you two talk while I call the doctor."

Tammy disappeared. And then a face edged with dark hair appeared right above her. Eyes like deep amber seemed to smile even though the line of his mouth never twitched, and he pressed a hand against the mattress next to her arm, never quite touching her. But she could feel his presence, his strength.

She let out a slow breath.

"De—" Her voice cracked, and he held up a hand to stop her.

"Please. It's Zach." Generous lips formed the words, but they seemed to take a long time to reach her ears. He spoke with a familiarity that she couldn't place. Was she supposed to know this man? "I've been looking forward to meeting you." Apparently not. Thank goodness. "I've been checking in on you every day. The doctor said you thumped your head pretty good, but the swelling has been going down."

How was she supposed to respond? "That's good…I guess."

"It is, indeed." His lip twitched, but he didn't give her more than half a smile. With a quick glance over his shoulder, he continued, "Do you feel up to answering a few questions?"

She wanted to shake her head, but then he'd come back and interrupt her sleep again. She really just wanted to drift back into oblivion where it had been warm and quiet. Where there'd been no pain and her stuttering thoughts were neither important nor questioned.

"Do you remember how you got here?"

She thought about it for a long moment. Blinking her only mobile eye—why wouldn't her other eye respond?—she tried to peek around the curtain in her mind, to reveal the corners she couldn't quite make out. The sheet wouldn't budge, and the harder she tried to move it, the more her head throbbed.

Finally she shook her head.

He scratched at the little point of his chin, his smile dimming for a brief moment, the lines at the corners of his eyes disappearing. "That's all right. We'll come back to it. You've been through a pretty big ordeal."

Oh, really? What had she been through that left her straining to uncover her memories and answering a strange detective's questions? He'd said that it was nice to meet her, but he'd come into her room like he belonged there. Clearly he'd been waiting for her to wake up, and Tammy had gone straight to him. But she wasn't expected to know him. Why did he seem to know her?

She wanted to ask, but the words just weren't there.

Zach brushed a wayward strand of dark brown hair off

his forehead with the back of his hand, plastering an easy grin in place. Really, it wasn't so much a smile as it was a visual encouragement, like if he kept looking at her like that she'd be able to get up right then and walk out of this room. "Let's try something a little easier. We've been calling you Julie Thomas because you were found in the park on Thomas Road across from Jack and Julie's Grill." So he didn't know her, and she wasn't supposed to recognize him. Relief washed over her like the bath she craved. "We didn't find your ID."

"It's in my purse." It was always in there.

He shook his head slowly. "We didn't find a purse, either."

She tried playing out all the movements she'd made before losing her bag. But she didn't even know where to start. And every possible step was blank. No context. No location. No memories.

"Maybe you can tell me your real name?"

She nodded slowly, controlling every movement to keep the pain from flaring up again. Of course she could. There were just some things a woman never forgot.

He lifted his thick eyebrows as though his anticipation grew with every tick of the clock.

Closing her eye and swallowing against the sandpaper in her throat, she opened her mouth and tried to form the word.

But it wasn't there.

The name she'd surely heard thousands of times floated just out of reach. Like the string on a balloon caught in the wind, it danced away until her lips sputtered and a tear leaked down her cheek.

Dear God, I don't even know my own name.

TWO

Zach hated to see a woman cry. More than he despised all-night stakeouts and stale doughnuts, he hated when a woman cried.

He cleared his throat, offering a low whisper. "Your name. Can you tell me your name?"

"I don't re-remember." Her words, broken by a soft sob, barely made it to his ears.

He swung another glance across the room to see if the nurse had heard the same thing that he had, but she had yet to return with the doctor.

Turning back to Julie, he leaned a little closer. Maybe he'd misunderstood. "You don't remember?"

She shook her head again, uneven brown locks falling just onto the white bandage taped to her forehead. "I'm not— I can't—" She looked away before blinking one watery eye filled with more questions than he could answer. A trembling reached her bottom lip, and she sank her perfectly straight teeth into it. But that wasn't enough to stop the returning tears from escaping closed lids. Moisture appeared even at the swollen seam of her left eye, still purple and red like an overripe strawberry.

Taking a deep breath, he did the only thing he could remember doing the handful of times Samantha had cried in his presence. With the tips of his fingers, he patted her forearm gingerly, avoiding the patch of road rash just below her elbow. She must have caught herself there because the scrape covered a good bit of real estate.

At his touch, Julie jerked her arm away, then squeaked as every muscle in her body tensed. The veins in her neck popped out, her lips pulling back to reveal clenched teeth.

"It'll be all right."

The words didn't hold much weight. How could they? The only person who could help him solve her case couldn't remember her own name. She was locked somewhere in her own mind, and he had yet to decipher a shred of evidence to help her fill in the missing pieces, to figure out who had left her beaten and on the brink of death.

The metal legs of the nearby chair scraped along the floor as he pulled it up to the bedside and slumped into it. Scrubbing a hand down his face, he rested his elbows on his knees, wrinkling the creases of his gray slacks.

"I can't see you."

He jumped up like her words had set the seat on fire and leaned over her bed, staring into her open eye. "Better?"

The muscles in her neck relaxed, and even the steady beat of her carotid artery seemed to settle from a frantic rhythm. She patted at her mattress until her fingers found his hand resting close by. She didn't exactly hold his hand. But she seemed to need the touch to confirm his proximity.

He didn't mind so much. Whatever he could do to help this girl. She sure needed it, and he felt somehow responsible for her. Of course, it wasn't his fault that she'd been attacked. But since rescuing her, he'd kept an eye out for any word of a missing person matching her description. Nothing yet.

Never taking her wary eye off of him, she said, "We

don't know each other. I mean, we didn't know each other. Before. Right?"

"That's right."

She coughed, the sound low and raspy like her throat was retaliating after not being used for so many days. Grabbing the pink plastic cup from the table, he pressed the straw to her lips, and she drank greedily.

When her gulps began to slow, he pulled the cup away and set it back on the rolling table. "Better?"

Only her eye moved to look in his direction. "No. I still can't remember my name." Her words were soft but filled to the brim with a pain he couldn't even imagine. She didn't sound bitter, just betrayed. Her mind refused to do what she needed it to—give her the information stored in it.

"It'll be okay." Another useless phrase. It promised something he couldn't back up. But there wasn't anything else to say, so he patted her hand.

"How did I end up here? What happened?"

He looked down at the spot where her fingers curled into his. She was clinging to anything that felt stable, and he didn't blame her. The nurse had told him to take it easy on Julie. Telling her the whole truth wasn't fair to her in this condition. It could send her reeling like a roller coaster. She didn't know that she'd been some lunatic's punching bag, that her face, covered with long, narrow bruises, suggested he'd used a pipe or other weapon. At least the doctor had confirmed that she hadn't been sexually assaulted, and all her internal organs—except her brain—were in good shape. It was her mind he was worried about, so he picked his words carefully. "I was kind of hoping you could tell me." He chuckled halfway, but she didn't respond in kind. She wasn't ready for that yet. "It looks like you got a pretty good knock on the head first. The doctor says you don't have any defensive wounds, so you were probably knocked unconscious right away."

She raised a hand to her cheek, covering one of her bruises, unspoken questions brimming in her eyes.

He nodded, confirming her injury. "But I'm not really sure what happened. We found you in Webster Park. Does that mean anything to you?"

She closed her eyes, finally offering only a tiny shake of her head.

He gave her fingers a little squeeze. "All right. We'll figure it out."

"We?" Her tone rose, laced with hope.

"You're my case. I'll see it through until it's solved, which means figuring out your name and where you belong."

"Thank you." Her words didn't make much of a sound, but he had no problem reading her lips. They weren't quite as white as they had been when he'd first laid eyes on her. In fact her whole face had gained some color, if not quite enough.

Well, he'd been hoping to start with her real name. But that wasn't going to happen today. Maybe there would be some good news back at the station. After seeing her safely to the E.R. on the night she'd been discovered, he'd immediately requested the footage from security cameras near the park. If those were in, maybe they'd have something telling. Or at least something to point him to the next step.

There were other ways of finding out her name. Like canvassing both of the Twin Cities with her picture. No. That was impractical. There had to be a better way to show her picture to thousands of people. Like in a newspaper. Or online. Or both.

He was about to ask if she'd be open to running a story

in the paper when a booming voice filled the room. "Well, well. Look who finally decided to wake up."

Julie cringed at the noise, her hand balling into a fist. "It's okay," he whispered. "Just the doctor." Who had no bedside manner.

Zach kept that last part to himself.

The silver-haired man in the white lab coat marched across the tiled floor, the nurse right behind him. The doctor didn't bother to introduce himself. He just started giving orders instead. "You need to go. You've waited around long enough, and now you're just adding to her stress. She doesn't need any of that right now."

Nodding, Zach pulled his hand away from hers. In a movement faster than he'd seen from her thus far, she scrambled her fingers until they clutched his.

"Will you come back?"

He paused just before stepping away, taking in the panic building in Julie's eye. He didn't begrudge her the fear. Even he couldn't be sure exactly how much danger she was in. By the light of day, he'd been able to make out the marks in the grass at the park, where she'd been dragged away from the street and into the shadow of the trees. Someone had wanted her permanently out of the picture.

Bending over so that she could clearly see his face, he gave her a slow wink. "Count on it."

Letting the door to the station swing closed behind him, Zach walked to his desk, falling into his chair, which rolled away from his computer under his weight. He walked his feet forward, until he was right where he needed to be— staring at a blank screen and wondering if that's what Julie felt like every waking minute.

He grabbed the phone and jabbed in the number he knew by heart.

"This is Tabby."

"It's Zach."

Tabitha let out a deep, throaty laugh. "To what do I owe this pleasure, Detective Jones?"

When people first met Tabby, they generally had a hard time believing that the sixty-year-old firecracker with a shock of white hair was *the* Tabitha Guster, Pulitzer-Prize-winning reporter for the *Star Tribune*.

Zach didn't have any trouble believing it, though. Tabby had been his mom's best friend since they were roommates at the University of Minnesota forty years ago. Tabby had become more family than friend, and as the reporter covering the police beat, she and Zach had spent plenty of family dinners talking cases.

But the last time they'd talked, he hadn't been able to give her any information about an ongoing investigation, and she'd been none too happy with him for it. Would she be willing to do him a favor now?

Better to start off easy than dive in headfirst. Every Minnesota boy raised in the Land of Ten Thousand Lakes knew to jump feetfirst the first time. This situation was no different. "How're you doing?"

"Just fine. And your mom and the family?" She was playing along. Tabby had almost certainly spoken to his mother more recently than he had.

"We're all doing very well."

"Glad to hear it." She paused, waiting for him to speak. When he didn't hop right in, she continued, "I have to interview the police chief in twenty minutes. Want to tell me what this is about? Or should I call you back later?"

He leaned an elbow on the desk and rested his chin in his hand. "I need your help."

"Oh?" Her voice jumped an octave. "Work or pleasure?"

"Work."

She laughed with the kind of giddy joy he'd expect from someone half her age. But the truth was that the police beat still made her heart thump a little harder. And as a detective in need of her help, he was at her mercy. "Whatcha got?"

"I need to identify a victim, and I was hoping you could help."

"Which one?"

He paused, questioning his decision. Maybe this was a bad idea. It wasn't too late to keep this out of the papers and off-line. But then how was he going to figure out who she was and why she'd been attacked? He'd been checking the missing-persons database every day, but still hadn't found anything. If no one noticed Julie was gone, then he had no clear indication of how much danger she might really be in. "The one from Webster Park. She woke up."

"And she can't tell you her own name?" Tabby laughed like it was a funny joke, but stopped at his grunt. "She has amnesia?" Her words ran together, her tongue moving faster than she could enunciate.

"Uh-huh."

Measured breaths were the only sound coming from the other end of the line. Finally she sighed. "What do you want me to do?"

Zach chewed on the inside of his cheek and scratched at his chin. "Any chance you could run an article and a picture? See if anyone can identify her?"

"You think this was a mugging?" She sounded hopeful, and he hated to dash that theory, but all the evidence pointed away from that simple of an explanation.

"Well, her purse was missing and hasn't been located yet. But she was wearing a gold tennis bracelet and diamond earrings that weren't touched."

"And?" Apparently she could hear the unstated question in the tone of his voice.

"And she was dragged about fifty yards into the park to conceal her body between trees."

A rush of air slipped through Tabby's lips. "I should guess not, then. And you think it's safe to run her picture? If we post it on our social media networks, it could be seen by anyone in a matter of minutes. You want her attacker to be aware that she can't remember her own name?"

"I don't know." He shoved his fingers through his hair, curling his fingers into a fist and pulling on it. Why couldn't this be an easy case? Nothing about it was black-and-white. Nothing was straightforward. Nothing really made much sense.

Then again, most of his cases started this way.

They just didn't usually start with a live victim.

Clearing his throat, he glanced at the blank computer screen. He had to do something to help Julie find her memories. Whatever it took.

"You run her prints?" Tabby asked.

"Of course. No hits on the regional database, and the feds said there's a backlog for IAFIS right now. Who knows how long it'll take? Two weeks. Maybe three. What if we don't have that long?" The Integrated Automated Fingerprint Identification System was the largest database of its type in the world. It was also managed by the FBI, and Zach had no clue where his case fit into the thousands of others looking for information from the system. Julie's case certainly wasn't at the top of their list, even if she was at the top of his.

"What if the dirtbag is still out there? How are you going to keep him from coming after her?"

"That's why I called the best writer in the state."

She laughed. "Don't go blowin' smoke, young man."

"Hey, if anyone could write up a story that conveniently

left out the details of her location without making it sound like that's exactly what they'd done, it's you."

After another chuckle, she agreed to meet Julie the next day. They hung up, but the tightness in his gut didn't alleviate.

He had to find Julie's real name and her family. Someone had to be looking for this girl. And after at least three days, they would know she was gone. Why hadn't she shown up among the listed missing yet?

He flipped on his monitor and the computer hummed to life. The keys on his keyboard clacked as he hammered on them, opening up the missing-persons database for the fifth time since that night in the park. He narrowed the search down by her age—about twenty-five. Except it wasn't easy to tell under all the scrapes and bruises. He widened it to anyone between the ages of twenty and forty just to be sure he wasn't missing her. He continued to narrow it down. Female. Caucasian. Long brown hair.

Well, it had been long when he'd found her. At the hospital they'd chopped off most of the hair in front to get a better look at that gash.

And those eyes. Enormous and brown like a doe's in spring.

The database searched its information, pulling from every corner of the state. Only two names reported missing within the past month popped up. AnnaBeth Doorsey, a thirty-nine-year-old mother of five from Duluth, and Elsie Sorenson, a twenty-one-year-old college student from Saint Paul.

Neither one looked like Julie.

Slamming his hand on his desk, he almost missed the sound of his name ringing through the bull pen. "Jones!"

He jerked out of his thoughts to stare at Lucas Ramirez, the new guy in Homicide. "What's up?"

"The chief got a call today from the U.S. Marshals Service, asking if we had any reports of missing kids or babies."

Zach stared at the man, squinting as he tried to shift his thoughts from the image of Julie in his mind. "Babies?"

"Yeah." Ramirez looked at his notepad and read from his scrawls there. "We don't have any active cases involving unidentified or missing kids right now, but the marshal who called, Serena Summers, said that they think there might be a Minneapolis connection to a witness they're protecting."

"Not that I know." Shaking his head, Zach turned back to the only two women who matched his search but didn't match his Julie. And then he added over his shoulder, "Any word on those security camera videos I requested?"

"Oh, yeah. I got those."

Zach jumped to his feet and took the discs from the younger man. "You look at these yet?"

"Just this one. From out in front of Jack and Julie's." Hope bubbled in his chest. Until Ramirez popped it. "Nothing on it from the night of the attack. The manager said the camera is on a rotating recording system. It was recording the back loading docks during the night delivery after ten."

Perfect. "What else did you get?"

"A few more restaurants, an ATM camera and the street camera from the corner of Thomas and Gavel."

Zach kept the videos from two restaurants and the street camera and handed the others back to the other detective. "Do you have time to take a look at these?"

"Are you just looking for the dark-haired girl who was attacked?"

"Yes. And anything else that seems unusual or out of place."

"Sure." Ramirez sat back down at his desk, sticking the first disc into his computer.

Zach matched his motions, settling in to watch the silent black-and-white clips. The first two videos showed nothing but the evening crowd, bustling in and out of popular restaurants near the park. The gaggle of men and women jumbled together and made any specific face or feature indistinguishable. Even when he slowed the images all the way down, he couldn't make out anything beyond gender.

After two hours, his eyes burned and head throbbed from staring so intently at his screen, hoping to see something he wasn't even sure was there. Rubbing the bridge of his nose, he got up and walked to the water fountain. Bending over, he took several long sips, then stretched his back as he returned to his upright position.

"You find anything?" he said as he strolled by Ramirez's desk.

"Nope. Nothing yet."

Zach nodded to show he'd heard the response, but his mind was already miles away in an almost deserted park. Maybe this was just a futile search.

He'd hit roadblocks in other cases, but he'd never felt quite so defeated so early into an investigation.

He'd just never had the image of such beautiful eyes seared in his mind, eyes that begged for his help. And the way she grabbed for his hand at the hospital, afraid he wouldn't return, clutched at his heart.

Shoving his third and final disc into his computer's player, he sighed. At least this camera, unlike the restaurant cameras, was angled toward the faces of the pedestrians, most of them walking toward their cars parked along Thomas Road. He sped up the video as the time stamp passed the dinner rush and through long periods without anyone using the crosswalk. The clock on the footage showed almost 2200 when a lone figure carrying some sort of case against her chest, with both arms wrapped around it, stopped at the corner.

He pushed his chair back and sat straight up in it before leaning closer to the screen. The figure looked like a woman with dark hair, and as she swung to look over her shoulder, her hair fanned out, long and just a little wavy.

Just about like Julie's the night that she'd been found.

On the screen, the woman jabbed at the crosswalk button several times, looking behind her twice before she finally ventured out into the road, checking for oncoming traffic from both directions. The light hadn't changed in her favor, but she still hurried into the street, pausing only to brush something from her cheek into the bag she was carrying.

And then she disappeared from the camera's view.

He rewound the scene and slowed it to a crawl and zoomed in on her. Frame by frame the figure moved across the street. And then she stopped for a fraction of a second and looked right into the camera.

Julie.

Even without the scrapes and black eye she now sported, there was no doubt this was her.

His stomach lurched. It was their first real clue. But what did it mean? Only that she'd been attacked sometime after ten o'clock that night.

And then she reached for her cheek.

He'd thought it was a hair in her way, but at the slower speed, he could clearly make out the five little fingers and the care with which she tucked the wayward hand back into the blanket in her arms.

"Ramirez? Do you have the number for that contact in the marshals' office you just told me about?"

"I think so." Papers rustled on the other desk, but Zach couldn't tear his gaze away from the woman looking directly into the street camera and carrying what was undoubtedly a baby.

Julie popped a piece of melon into her mouth, set her fork back on her dinner tray and picked up the newspaper for the tenth time, staring hard at the picture on the front of the section. Who was the woman gazing back at her?

She knew that it was her own likeness. After all, Tabby Guster had taken the photo when she'd stopped by the day before. Zach had told her this could help them identify her and begin to put the pieces of her life back together. She'd been only too eager to agree.

But now that she stared at the square chin, full lips, brown eyes and pixie cut that she didn't recognize, it tore at her insides.

How could she not even know her own features? How could they be so foreign when they were literally at the tip of her nose?

With a finger she traced the short hair in the photograph then touched the real hair at her temple. The nurse said they'd cut off a lot of it that first night. But Julie didn't have anything to compare it to.

The disposable cell phone that Zach had left with her let out a low hum as it scooted across the table at her bedside. Setting the paper down, she scooped it up. "Hello?"

"Hey, it's Zach."

"Hi." She twisted to catch a glimpse of the clock on the adjacent wall. It was after eleven. "Are you still on duty?"

"No. Why?"

"Oh. It's just kind of late—"

He sucked in a sharp bite of air. "Did I wake you? I'm sorry."

"No. Not at all. I was just— I'm just looking at the article in the paper. Again." Oh, why did she add that? She sounded like she was so interested in herself that she couldn't stop reading about the woman without her memory.

"It's a good article." He paused for a long time, but she could tell he wanted to say more. Finally he filled it in. "It's a pretty picture."

Where her self-berating had just been, warmth filled her chest at his compliment. And with it a bit of trepidation. She wasn't used to being complimented like that. At least she didn't think she was.

He cleared his throat, effectively turning the conversation to less awkward ground and relieving her of the pressure of finding an appropriate response. Thank goodness.

"I was actually calling to let you know that we've gotten a couple tips from the hotline."

"Already? Did you find out who I am?" The smile that tugged on her mouth refused to go away, growing as fast as the hope blooming in her heart.

"Not yet. But there are a few that we're going to follow up on and see if anything pans out."

Like a leaking balloon, hope escaped, leaving a weight heavy on her shoulders.

"Thanks for letting me know."

"We'll figure out who you are. I promise."

His words were kind, but were they really in his control? She replayed them as she hung up the phone and leaned back against her pillows with closed eyes. She needed help beyond this world. God was going to have to heal her brain and restore her memories, or she might always be Julie Thomas—not who she really was.

A squeaking wheel jerked her out of her reverie, and she glanced up just as a large blond man in a maintenance uniform rushed across her room. He'd left his mop and yellow bucket sitting by the door, which he'd closed behind him.

She tried to wave him off. "I don't need anything."

But he ignored her, and before she could make sense of his presence, he reached her bedside, pressed his meaty hands to her throat and squeezed.

THREE

Julie tried to scream, but no breath could pass through her constricted airway. The pressure on her throat made her eyes water and her chest burn. Darkness clouded the corners of her vision, but she fought the temptation to succumb to its sweet release.

And she fought the man standing next to her bed, the man who was causing her agony.

All she could see were his broad shoulders and beefy arms, his face just out of her line of sight, but she clawed at him, digging her nails into every bit of flesh she could find. As she raked her fingers down his arm, he growled and yanked his hand away from her throat before hitting the elastic bandage covering the brace around her arm with his fist.

Every point from her wrist to her elbow screamed at the abuse, but she pushed it from her mind, gasping for oxygen before he pressed against her air pipe again.

He leaned in closer, but she could still only see his blond hair, wrinkled forehead and squinty eyes, the lines at the corners taut with the effort it took to keep her from flying out of the bed. She kicked and pushed and tried to scream, but again, there was no sound.

Grasping for the nurse's call button near her waist, her

fingers caught only the very edge before her attacker shoved it to the floor, the plastic landing with a sharp report on the tile floor.

She needed a weapon. Something. Anything to make him back off long enough for her to catch a breath and call for help.

And still the darkness called, willing her to just close her eyes and drift off to sleep, whispering that this fight wasn't one she could win.

But she had something to live for. She did.

She just didn't know what it was.

With jerking motions, she patted her chest and stomach, hoping to find a scalpel or a pair of scissors or a syringe. Her search came up empty, and she flailed her arms until her uninjured hand connected with the side table holding the dinner tray she'd picked at all evening. The metal lid clanged as it bounced off the wall and reverberated when it reached the floor. If she could just get a hold of the edge of the tray, maybe she could hit him in the side of the head. But her fingers couldn't find a purchase on the rounded edge, and it, too, slipped from her grasp, clattering to the floor.

As the suffocating pressure below her chin increased, she swiped her hand over the table one more time. And then she found just what she needed.

A fork.

Clutching the handle in her fist, she swung it at his arm with as much force as she could muster. When the tines broke skin, she pressed it farther into his arm before yanking it back and stabbing him again.

"Ow!" he screamed, as if she wielded a dagger.

She plunged it into his arm, and his fingers loosened. Gulping air, she jabbed at him over and over, puncturing skin and pulling out every time.

She wasn't seriously injuring him, but it couldn't feel much better than a bee sting.

Finally he let go altogether, and she had the freedom to let loose the blood-curdling yell that had been trapped. It filled the room, went right through the door, flooded the hallway and was promptly followed by a ruckus outside her room that would have brought her out of a coma.

She knew Brad, her night nurse, was on his way just by the rhythm of his feet on the floor by the nurses' station. And his steps were not alone. But her attacker vanished. He kicked the mop bucket by the door and it sloshed water, which fell onto the floor with a clap, a sweet pine scent filling the room. The chatter of a handful of high-pitched voices demanding to know what had happened reached her long before she could make out their forms.

"Who was that coming out of your room?"

"What happened?"

As Brad reached her bedside, she held a shaking hand out to him, needing the stability and support that she'd come to expect from the only other man in her life for the moment, but Brad didn't reach out to her. Instead he picked up the end of her IV tube, which had pulled free during the struggle, and looked at the mess. Leaking saline had left a trail from her stomach down the side of the bed and halfway across the floor.

Where was Zach? He'd know what to do. He'd know how to make her trembling stop.

"What happened?" Brad asked again, his words nearly drowned out by the pounding of her heart in her ears.

"Call security." Her words came out on a wheeze, and she sucked in air as fast as she could. "That man attacked me. Tried to—" She pointed at her throat. "Tried to strangle me."

Brad's eyes grew wide, if a little doubtful. "Are you sure?"

Hadn't he seen the man running down the hall? She nodded, pushing herself up on her elbow and ignoring the pain that sliced down her arm.

He snatched up the phone and punched in a few numbers before telling the person on the other end to send up security and have them check the back stairwell and exits for a man with blond hair in a blue maintenance uniform. Two female nurses hovering in the doorway followed suit, hurrying in the direction of the attacker's hasty exit.

As Brad's voice chirped on, Julie sank back against the elevated bed. The rush of adrenaline had vanished, stealing her strength.

"I'll be right back to get you cleaned up, Julie. Security is on its way." Brad turned to go, but she grabbed at his arm.

"Call Zach. Please."

"Who?"

"Detective Jones. Tell him…tell him I need him."

Zach jabbed the hospital's elevator button three times, probably harder than it required to light up, but he didn't have time to wait for it. When the doors didn't open, he abandoned the lift and ran into the stairwell, taking them two at a time for three flights before running down the corridor.

His breathing was rapid and painful by the time he reached the ICU. The night nurses shot him strange looks, but the big guy, the one who had called him, waved him toward the security guard in a black uniform.

"Tell me what happened." His words were sharp, like the smack of a hammer against wood.

The security guard had pimples and a patchy beard. He wasn't much more than a kid with a walkie-talkie and a flashlight, and he took two steps back at Zach's approach. "Umm. Got here as fast as I could when I got the call, but the guy had already vanished. We checked the back stairwell, and he's not there, either." The kid wrung his hands and looked toward the ceiling tiles. "I guess he's long gone."

"When did you get the call?"

Zach could almost see him calculating the time as he stared at his watch through narrowed eyes. "I guess about twenty minutes ago?"

He let out a short breath, jamming his hands onto his hips. "Can you be more specific?"

The kid shrugged and shook his head.

"You can go." Zach dismissed the guard but couldn't seem to take the single step required to enter Julie's room. Straightening his shoulders, he tried to prepare himself for whatever he might see. Brad wouldn't have been so calm on the phone if she'd been severely injured. But he'd said she needed Zach.

It had at once exhilarated and terrified him.

He liked being needed. He liked taking care of people who couldn't take care of themselves. Except Julie was an unknown. Nothing about her or her situation was certain or easy.

And he couldn't stay away from her.

He strolled across the room, his shoes silent against the tile. She was so small beneath the blanket, her feet not even close to reaching the end of the mattress. The bed was angled so she was partially sitting up, but her eyes were closed, as though she was fast asleep. Maybe he should go. Let her get some real rest after another traumatic event.

But she'd asked for him.

At her side he rested a hand on her arm. She was so pale. Her face and lips were nearly white, the only real color a ring of yellow already materializing at her throat and the still purple bruises.

Her good eye fluttered open, and her swollen one even managed a slit through which he could make out a matching brown iris. The corners of her lips shifted into a low-wattage smile. "You came."

"The nurse said you needed me."

Her eyes drifted closed again, and she bit both her top and bottom lips until they disappeared. "I did—do."

"All right. I'm here." He brushed a strand of hair out of her eye, but jerked his hand back immediately. That was way more than professional, and he couldn't afford to be anything but with a victim. He had to rein in any wayward feelings and get down to business. "You want to tell me what happened?"

"I must have seen or done something pretty incredible."

He lifted his eyebrows, but she continued without any other prodding.

"He still wants me dead."

She spoke with such certainty and calm, yet every muscle in his body tensed, every hair on the back of his neck stood on end. She was in danger. And it was his mistake. If he hadn't suggested the newspaper article, her attacker might still believe his work was done.

He swallowed the guilt that rose in his throat. "I'm sorry. This is my fault." Every syllable threatened to choke him, each one harder than the last.

Her eyebrows rose, the top of her nose wrinkling as she stared at him. "Funny. You don't look much like the guy who was in here before."

"You know what I mean. I promised I'd take care of you. And instead I inadvertently led that guy right to you."

She shook her head, shifting her arm out from under his hold, and his fingers immediately missed the absence of her warmth. Until she slipped her hand into his and squeezed. A breathy sigh escaped, her shoulders relaxing into the pillow. "It wasn't in the paper. Tabby didn't say where I was." With the lift of her sprained wrist and the wave of a single finger, she halted his intended interruption. "If he was watching the paper, he would've noticed there wasn't a story about me. About my body being found. He knew I was alive. And he would have found me eventually."

His heart thudded twice and then returned to a normal rhythm. She was absolutely right. But the guilt still poked and prodded his insides, leaving him sore, as if he'd taken a hockey puck to the gut.

"And he'll come looking for me again."

She was so matter-of-fact about it that he choked on his own breath, coughing and sputtering while she stared at him out of one eye. Of course, she was right. Someone certainly wanted her dead, so why didn't she look more scared?

The fingers in his grip began a slow tremor, quaking even more with every rise and fall of her chest. This was her fear in physical form. Her face showed no sign, but her hand trembled. While wearing a facade of confidence, she revealed the truth only to him. She was terrified.

And he had to scare her even more.

Whoever they were dealing with had disappeared. Right along with a baby she'd been carrying.

"You're not in this alone." The words were out before they were even fully formed in his mind, and he backed them up with a gentle smile.

She turned her head away to face the closed blinds over a window that looked out on the parking lot. Her eyes were closed, and for a moment, he wondered if she'd fallen asleep. But then she whispered so softly that he had to bend all the way over to hear her words.

"What if I'm not who you think I am? What if I deserved this?"

What was going on inside that barren mind of hers? Her forgotten memories provided a breeding ground for fear to fester. With no truth to combat the lies, they easily stole her peace. She needed someone to remind her that she was a good woman with a kind heart.

He could do that. He wanted to do that.

Letting go of her hand, he walked around the end of the bed until he could squat so his face was right in her line of vision.

"Look at me, Julie."

One lid slowly lifted, her pupil dilating until it seemed to blend with the darker circles in the outer rings of her eye.

"First of all, no one deserves something like this. No one. Do you understand me?"

She nodded.

"Second, you're not a criminal. No matter what you can't remember, the core of your heart, the person you are deep down, is still there."

She nibbled on the corner of her bottom lip, her eyebrows pulling together to make three little lines above her nose. "How can you be so sure?"

"I see it in the way you treat people and the way you reach for my hand when you need something stable." She let out a little laugh, half embarrassment and half uncertainty. "You trust me, and I trust you. Criminals don't trust cops." Then he added a little wink. "Plus, I ran your fingerprints. If you'd committed a crime anywhere in the state of Minnesota, I'd know about it."

Her laugh this time was hearty if a bit hoarse. "Thank you."

"I'm just sorry that he found you. But I swear, I won't let it happen again. We'll find him and you'll be safe."

He liked being right at her level as emotions flickered in her eye, first relief, then uncertainty and finally resignation. She didn't have a choice but to see this through. But maybe knowing she wasn't facing it alone helped her to find some strength.

He stood, and her eye grew wide. "You're not leaving, are you?" The pitch of her voice rose, her hand clenched into a fist around the brace and bandage between her thumb and forefinger.

"I was just going to grab a chair. My legs will fall asleep if I stay in that position too long. All right?"

A chagrined smile fell into place as she nodded. But her grin was immediately broken by a yawn that cracked her jaw.

As he carried the chair from the corner, the urge to ask her about the baby he'd seen in the security video battled with the voice telling him that she needed rest. If she heard about a missing baby, she wasn't going to get a minute of sleep. He needed her mind fresh and prepared to remember anything that might surface when the U.S. Marshals arrived.

Still the voice that demanded to know the whereabouts of the missing child poked at the back of his mind.

He didn't have to cannonball into the question. He could dip a toe in. He could just check the temperature.

Sitting down, he was almost directly on her level again. Her eyelid had drooped, the lines of tension on her face vanished in the peace near sleep.

"Julie?"

"Hmm?" The sound was little more than a hum in the back of her throat, her eyelashes barely fluttering against pale cheeks. For the first time, he noticed a path of freckles running across her nose. They were close together on her nose but turned sparse as they reached her cheeks. She embodied both the innocence of youth and the fear that was very adult. And it twisted into his stomach.

"I got a call today from a marshal, who is interested in your case. She wants to talk with you tomorrow."

Her brows furrowed, eyes still closed. "About what?" Her tongue sounded thick, like every word was a fight to get out.

He pressed his finger and thumb around his mouth, scraping at the dark shadow growing there. "I'm not sure exactly. She wonders if you might be able to recognize someone that she's been investigating. I suppose she wants to know everything you know."

"Ha." There was genuine humor in her shallow laugh. "That's not much these days."

A smile that matched hers fell into place for just a moment. Wouldn't it be nice to be able to just laugh with her? But it would do neither of them any good so long as someone was after her and a baby was missing. "Julie, do you remember anything else about that night?"

"Like what?"

He let out a slow breath, praying for the words that would neither frighten nor mislead. "Were you alone that night? Was there anyone else with you?"

The shallow rise and fall of her chest stopped for a long heartbeat. "I can't remember anything." And then just before her breaths turned deep with sleep, she sighed. "Yet."

FOUR

Zach slammed his car door behind him, hustling between parked vehicles toward the hospital doors. Checking his watch, he pulled on his jacket as he reached the main entrance. The deserted main entrance. He was supposed to meet the marshals there at ten-thirty. He'd been running a little late, but maybe they had been, too.

Maybe they wouldn't show at all.

Was it wrong that he'd been hoping for that all morning? He just couldn't shake the suspicion that this interview wasn't best for Julie. He was almost certain it would be useless for Serena Summers and her partner.

Just as he straightened his tie and ducked his head inside to make sure they weren't waiting for him there, a nondescript navy blue sedan pulled into the parking lot. It angled into the nearest parallel lines before both the driver's-side and passenger doors popped open.

A tall guy with dark, wind-tossed hair stepped out from behind the wheel. He wore a dark gray suit and a pressed white shirt, his shoulders pushing at the seams of his coat and not because he was excessively brawny. He had a sturdy build, and he walked with his chin high and back straight. That had to be McCall. Serena had said she was bringing her partner with her.

Serena—all graceful movements and willowy lines—
met up with McCall at the front of the car. She stepped in
front of him when the passage was too narrow for them to
walk side by side, and the big guy's eyes never left her form.
It wasn't an outright assessment of his partner, but there
was something in his eyes that revealed a strong emotion
between them. Maybe it was just respect.

Maybe not.

Zach stepped from beneath the cement overhang to greet
them. Reaching out to shake the thin woman's hand, he
said, "Marshal Summers?"

She had a firm grip and an easy smile. "Call me Serena."
Nodding her head, she indicated the man at her side. "This
is my partner, Josh McCall."

McCall's shake was even tighter than Serena's had been,
but it wasn't uncomfortable. Zach gave back as good as he
got, and a flicker of admiration appeared in the other man's
eyes, if only for a second.

"Zach Jones, Minneapolis P.D."

"Good to meet you." Josh let go and put his hand into
his pocket, hunching his shoulders against the brisk early
spring wind.

Serena's eyes shifted toward the sliding glass door, but
Zach didn't move to lead them inside to his witness. To his
Julie. First, he had questions that required answers. And
the hospital waiting room wasn't the place to find any kind
of privacy.

"I know you're eager to talk with Julie, but you should
know that she doesn't have any memory of the night she
was attacked."

Josh and Serena shared a quick look, their eyes meeting
in a flash and tearing apart just as quickly. Josh cleared his
throat, but it was Serena who spoke. "None at all?"

Shaking his head, he frowned. "As of two o'clock this

morning, she can't remember a thing. Including that she was carrying a baby the night that she was attacked. And I haven't told her about that yet."

Two sets of eyebrows rose in unison before Josh responded. "You know that'll have to come up today, right?"

A gust of wind picked up Serena's long ponytail, whipping it back and forth over her shoulder. She wrestled it back into place with her free hand, the other clutching a brown folder to her chest.

Shivers ran down Zach's arms, the cold stealing its way to his skin, joining the doubts bombarding his mind. He wanted to find the missing baby just like the marshals, but would telling Julie about the child really do anyone any good? He battled a vision of her terrified features when she learned what he'd seen in the video. She'd be horrified to discover that a baby had gone missing from her care. That kind of emotional trauma could just be a setback on her road to healing—and to ultimately uncovering what really happened that night.

Whether Zach's doubts played across his face or she was a pro at reading people, Serena leaned toward him. Her movement was barely a few inches, but it caught and held his attention. "I bet you've become pretty close to your witness." Her voice was low and a little husky. "We don't want to scare her, but we're dealing with something bigger than one missing child."

He'd figured as much.

Josh didn't bother changing his body language, his stance firm and unmoving. "We just need to ask her a few questions. Your witness—"

"She's a victim." At Zach's interruption, Josh's chin snapped up, so Zach continued, "She's not just the only witness, she was beaten to within an inch of her life. She can't recall her name or where she lives or who her family is." His words picked up speed as his pulse did the same. "As if one attack wasn't enough, someone snuck into her hospital room last night and tried to kill her again."

Almost certainly Serena's training and experience were the only things keeping her jaw from flapping open at his declaration. Her eyes were bright with the revelation of the second attack, and she held her packet even tighter below her chin. "Is she all right?"

"She'll be okay. The doctor said there was no permanent damage. But I hope you can see why I'm hesitant to add to her emotional strain, especially knowing that she hasn't been able to remember anything, and this is probably all a dead end."

Josh caught Serena's gaze yet again, his eyebrows pinching together as he pressed his hands deeper into his pockets. "So she saw someone last night?"

"Ye-es." Zach dragged the word out, not quite sure where Josh was going with his line of questions.

"So she could identify him?"

"Yes. She could probably pick him out of a lineup or identify a mug shot."

Serena's smile dipped, turning grim as her brown eyes squinted directly at him. She had to be picking up on his hesitation. As silence hung over their small group, she rubbed her chin and glanced at the ground.

Josh watched her closely, his stance alert, but he held back, letting her take the lead, despite a nearly palpable tension radiating from him.

"Zach, it's imperative that we talk with your witness. We have to know as much information as she can give us. There are lives on the line—babies are disappearing."

Babies.

His gut clenched. Hard. This was bigger than the missing baby he was already looking for. And he couldn't look himself in the mirror if he didn't do everything in his power to help those kids.

With his hands on his hips, he asked, "What's going on?"

The marshals glanced at each other again, and Josh gave a quick nod before speaking. "Serena and I have been keeping tabs on a man named Don Saunders."

Josh paused, as though waiting for any reaction from Zach. "Never heard of him."

"Don was arrested in connection to a murder and was being transported for questioning in police custody near Saint Louis, but a couple of his buddies staged a car accident, and he escaped."

Zach sucked in a harsh breath. Letting a suspect escape could shatter an officer's confidence. Being a cop was hard enough when everything was going right. But a man could drive himself crazy wondering what he could have done differently.

Poor guy.

But what did this have to do with Julie and missing babies?

Serena seemed to be able to read his mind, answering the question before he could ask it. "Other marshals tracked Don down in Denver, where they found him about to board a plane with an unidentified child. We still haven't been able to locate the baby's parents or figure out where she came from.

"Don escaped again before we could figure out what was going on, but we were able to locate Sam Wilson, one of the guys who helped to set up the last break. At first he was pretty closemouthed, but after a few weeks in custody, he folded like a hot dog bun, revealing that he'd been working with a man named Frank Adams to stage the car accident. According to Sam, Frank has a place pretty close to this area, although we don't know exactly where."

Like dominoes tumbling down in a row, the pieces of the story all fell into place. Zach nodded slowly, crossing his arms over his chest to keep the edges of his jacket from whipping around in the breeze. "So you figure that a missing baby near Frank's known hideout might have a connection to this Don Saunders." He didn't bother phrasing it as a question, and Serena's slow nod confirmed his assessment of the situation.

"We're running out of leads to follow up on." Josh tugged at his earlobe, hunching his shoulders. "This is the best tip we've got."

Zach couldn't stop a humorless chuckle from escaping. "A woman who doesn't know her own name is your best lead?"

With mirrored smiles, Josh and Serena nodded. "It may be a long shot, but if Julie can identify Frank in any way, then we can confirm he is—or at least was recently—in the area. And then we know who we're looking for."

All right. There was no way to protect Julie from this questioning. And when she knew the truth about the missing child, she'd pummel her own mind to unearth the details and solve the disappearance.

As he led the marshals into the busy hospital, Zach shot up a quick prayer that this meeting would lead to the location of the missing baby and not derail any progress Julie had made thus far.

Julie leaned against her bed, the muscles in her legs trembling after the short walk across the room. She'd barely splashed water on her face, combed her new hairstyle and checked out the swelling around her eye before her strength had vanished. But she'd pushed herself to get back across the room. No way did she want the nurse—or Zach— finding her in a heap on the bathroom floor.

"Julie?"

She yanked the belt of her robe tighter at her waist before looking up into Zach's face. But he wasn't alone. Grabbing the lapels, she pulled them together beneath her chin, never taking her gaze off the tall man and slender woman standing just behind Zach.

He hustled across the room, cupping her elbow and helping her slide back onto her bed, her slippered feet dangling just above the floor.

"Are you all right? You look really pale." His grip on her arm loosened, but he didn't back away.

She nodded slowly. "I'm okay." Her gaze traveled back to the couple still in the doorway. Her questions must have shown on her face, as Zach didn't wait for her to ask them before answering.

"These are the U.S. Marshals I told you about last night." A quick glance over his shoulder had the woman walking quickly across the room, her hand outstretched.

"Serena Summers." Her grip was gentle around Julie's brace, but her smile didn't quite wrinkle the fine lines at the edge of her eyes. "And this is my partner, Josh McCall."

The man strode toward them, his gaze even and detached. No, that wasn't quite right. He was engaged but calm, a shield of professionalism blocking his true emotions.

Julie wrapped her arms around her middle. Maybe she could just crawl back into bed and pull the covers over her head. Whatever they wanted with her, she couldn't give it to them. It certainly would require remembering more than that her face didn't usually look like it had been used as a punching bag.

But that was all she had at the moment.

And only God knew how much longer it would be that way. The doctor had said he didn't think it was a permanent condition, but he couldn't pinpoint when her memory would return.

Until then she wouldn't be much help to anyone.

Zach dropped his hand, and she immediately missed the warmth. "The marshals think that you might have come into contact with someone that they're searching for."

She shrugged and shook her head. "Do you think the man you're looking for is the one who attacked me? I can't remember anything from before that night."

"Detective Jones filled us in on your condition. I'm so sorry. But we hope you might be able to help us."

How was she supposed to respond to that? She was sorry about it, too. It didn't change the reality.

"We'd appreciate it if you'd take a look at a headshot to see if you recognize him." Serena snapped the elastic tie from around her file and flipped through the pages within.

Julie looked at Zach, who nodded slowly, his eyes bright with hope and encouragement. "All right. I'll try."

Serena held out a five-by-seven image, the man in the picture standing against the evenly spaced height lines of a police wall, a black plaque at his chest announcing his name as *Adams, Frank*. His hair was dark and ruffled, maybe beginning to gray at the temples. He had narrow-set eyes that looked almost black, but it could have been just a shadow. The bridge of his nose zigged and zagged, clearly broken at least twice. Thin lips were nearly hidden behind a five o'clock shadow, which could do nothing to camouflage the pink scar that slashed across his chin. It ran from the corner of his mouth toward the center of his jaw, perhaps a reminder of a fight gone terribly wrong.

She squinted and leaned forward, bringing the image closer to her face.

Did she remember those features? Was the scar or crooked nose familiar?

Waiting for the familiar sense of recognition to flood her mind, she didn't dare shift her gaze away.

But it never came.

Instead, a sinking sensation carried her stomach to her toes and she pressed her hand against the recently vacated spot. Looking up into Zach's tense features, she shook her head. "If I've ever seen him before, I don't remember." Handing the picture back to Serena, she continued, "I'm sorry. His face doesn't ring any bells."

The marshal tucked the image back into her folder, her eyebrows pinched together. She glanced at her partner, who crossed his arms over his chest, then seemed to think better of his stance, instead letting his hands drop to his sides and find their way into his pockets.

"What about the guy who attacked you here in the hospital last night? Could it have been him?" Zach slipped a hand into hers, squeezing her fingers until she met his gaze.

She closed her eyes, reliving that horrifying moment when she'd thought she'd never be able to breathe again. "No." Zach offered a reassuring squeeze in her pause, and she ran her free hand over her butchered locks very slowly. "The man last night had light hair, and his eyes weren't as dark."

"You're sure?"

She chewed on her lip and stared toward the ceiling for a long moment. Her mind had been letting her down for days now, and she found it difficult to trust even the few memories she'd made since waking up here at the hospital. What if it wasn't recalling the right details from the night before?

No. The man last night had had a narrow face and pale eyes. She was sure of it.

Almost.

"No. Yes." Something prickled at the back of her eyes,

and she pinched them closed to fight the building moisture. "I don't know."

Zach rubbed the back of her wrist with a gentle motion, making figure eights with his forefinger. "It's okay. Just do the best you can." When she looked up from the movements of his finger, she found his eyes filled with compassion, a worried frown puckering the skin between his eyebrows.

"I'm pretty sure that the man here wasn't the man in your picture. I'm sorry I couldn't be more help." She leaned against her pile of pillows, letting her eyes droop.

Walking across the room and trying to remember an unknown face had sapped her energy. At least the interview was over. It was time for a nap.

But the marshals had another question. "Julie, were you alone the night that you were attacked?" This from Josh, who met her gaze with kindness but an intensity that she could not fathom.

"You mean, was I with Frank Adams? I don't know." She let out a quick sigh. "I—I don't think so. But I don't know anything for sure."

"Not Frank. Was there anyone else with you before your attack?"

"Who?"

Zach ran a hand over his face but didn't release her fingers from his grip.

"I was with someone." The words rushed forward on a breath, a strange combination of question and certainty, followed immediately by a hiccup. With trembling fingers she wiped a hair off her forehead. "Who was I— How do you know?"

Serena opened her mouth, but Zach shot the marshal a look and cut in. "You were caught on a security camera a couple blocks from Webster Park."

"What? What was on it? What did it show? I wasn't alone?"

He nodded.

Her breathing lost all rhythm, every inhalation a surprise, every exhalation too fast. "Who was it? Who was I with? Was I with Frank?"

"No." Zach jabbed his fingers through his hair and closed his eyes, as though he didn't want to see her reaction when he told her the truth. "You were carrying a baby."

"A baby?" The words whisked around her mind, making almost no sense. They were testing her, trying to see what she remembered. She couldn't have had a child with her. Could she? She pressed a hand to her stomach. "My baby? Do I have a baby?" Her voice rose with each word until it filled the room, carrying down the hallway. "I'd remember if I had a baby, wouldn't I?"

Pressing a palm against her cheek, Zach forced her to meet his gaze, despite her rapid blinking. "We don't believe it's yours. Your doctor said you show no signs of having given birth in the last year."

Her breathing slowed as tears rushed to the forefront. Maybe they were from relief. "It's not mine." More likely they were from fear. "But where is it? What happened to it?"

"We were hoping you could tell us that."

FIVE

"I don't remember carrying a baby."

Zach held his breath as Julie's grip on his hand tightened. Her arms trembled, and he tried to hold steady, giving her every bit of strength he could, but the disbelief in her voice shook him to the core.

With pinched eyes and whispered words, she continued, "I can't— It's all a blank." The vibrato in her last word was a witness to the truth and the fear of the unknown. The unremembered. "Are you sure that it was me? Maybe it was someone else with a baby. Why would I be carrying a baby that isn't mine?"

Big brown eyes pleaded with him to say that there had been a mix-up. But he'd seen the video himself. He'd watched it at least half a dozen times.

There could be no mistake. It was Julie. And she was carrying a now-missing child.

His heart burned. More accurately, the spot just below his sternum roiled with the pain that the quick shake of his head must have caused her. "It's not a mistake."

She slipped her hand out of his, the chill it left reaching far below his skin. "I don't know why you were carrying a baby. But we'll figure it out. Together."

"It just doesn't make any sense. What happened to it?

Is—is it my fault that the baby is gone? Do you think I had something to do with the disappearance?"

Serena and Josh gave each other a knowing look, one that Julie didn't miss.

"You do! You think I had something to do with this whole thing. You think I took that baby." There were no questions in the deluge, just her eyes growing wider and filling with tears as the realization sank in.

This was not going well. Holding up his hands, palms facing out, he said, "Whoa. No one is accusing you of anything. We're all on the same team, looking for the same missing child."

Josh gave a reluctant dip of his chin, as much of an agreement as they were going to get from him. "Are you sure you can't remember? Anything would help. A face? A location? A name?" Josh's tone went beyond an unsolved case and missing children. Of course he cared about finding the kids, but there was something deeper, something more, something personal about this case. Desperation rang in his every word. And it added to the terrible weight that hunched Julie's shoulders and wrinkled her brow.

"Of course she's sure. She's already told you that." His response more terse than he'd anticipated, Zach let out a long sigh and plowed his fingers through his hair. "I'm sorry."

Serena stepped in front of Josh, offering Julie a gentle smile. "I know this is scary, but if you remember anything, we need to know as soon as possible." She pulled a business card from her coat pocket and held it out until Julie took it with shaking fingers. "Please call me if there's any change. All right?"

Julie nodded slowly, sinking against the pillow at the inclined head of the bed.

"I'll walk you out." Zach followed the marshals out of

the room, down the hall and into the elevator, but no one said a word until they stepped back outside, into the relative privacy of the deserted entrance.

"I'm guessing you know what my hunch is." Josh broke the silence, and his eyes didn't waver as he delivered the line.

"I know. But I don't agree. She's not working with Frank or whoever took that baby. She can't be."

Although her facial features were softer, Serena's tone was no less firm. "How can you be so sure?"

Good question. And it should have an easy answer, but somehow he knew that a gut instinct wouldn't convince these professionals. How about the look of trust in her eyes when he was near? That probably wouldn't do it, either. What about the quickening of his heart every time he saw her? Were they proof that Julie wasn't mixed up with a man possibly connected to at least one missing child and maybe more? Unfortunately not. They were nothing more than an indication that he was invested in solving this case.

Pushing his hands into his pockets, he stared at the underside of the overhang for a long moment. "If she's working with or for Frank Adams, why did someone try to kill her last night?"

"Tying up loose ends."

Zach shrugged. Josh had a point. "Maybe. But her prints aren't anywhere in the system."

Serena's eyebrows rose. "Even the national database?"

"Well, I'm not sure on that. I'm still waiting to hear back on IAFIS. There was a backlog. Maybe you could do something to help speed that along?"

Josh rubbed his flat palms together. "We'll see what we can do."

"I'd be grateful. And until we can confirm or deny Julie's story, I'll keep an eye on her and an eye out for Frank.

If she *was* working for him, he may be looking for her. For one reason or another." The thought made his skin crawl. If Adams was somehow connected to Julie's case—or with those missing kids—Zach would do anything to get his hands on the other man and make sure that he paid for whatever he'd done. "I'll work this case until it's solved, no matter if or how Frank Adams is involved."

Josh extended his hand. "We'll keep looking for that missing child, too. Keep us in the loop on your side of things?"

"You got it." Zach shook the offered hand and nodded at Serena, who waved.

"Thank you for your time."

As the marshals walked across the parking lot, Zach stared up at the puffy white clouds rolling across the sky. "We could sure use a little help down here. Would You mind giving Julie back her memory?" He waited for a flash of lightning or something to indicate that God was answering with an immediate affirmative, but after several long seconds with no visible response, he tucked his hands back into his pockets and nodded. "Would You take care of that baby then until we can find it?"

Peace settled over him as he spun and walked back into the hospital. And if he wore serenity like a coat when he returned to Julie's room, she was shrouded in a cloak of panic. Tears streamed down her cheeks; her red-rimmed eyes darted back and forth, searching for any history she could grasp.

He settled onto the edge of her bed and reached for her hand, which she had twisted into the top sheet. Pressing it between his palms, he watched her face closely until she met his gaze. Her mouth opened and closed, as she clearly struggled to find the words she wanted.

"It's going to be all right," he said again.

"How can you say that? How do you know that?" The volume of her words rose, carrying to the corners of the room, her free hand just as animated. "What if I really am working with that…that Frank guy? What if I am a criminal?"

"Okay." He squeezed his hands together, surrounding hers until her eyes no longer looked like they belonged to a hunted deer. "Take a deep breath." She followed his lead, in through the nose and out through the mouth, shoulders rising and falling in easy succession.

"Good. Now listen to me very carefully. Unless you've been making calls to him sometime in the last three days, you are not currently working with 'that Frank guy.' You're not currently breaking any laws, and if ten years on the force has taught me anything, you weren't breaking them before your attack."

Long lashes fell against her cheeks, and she shook her head. "How can you be so sure?"

"Easy. Perps don't become friends with cops."

She peeked at him, hope tugging at the corners of her pink lips. "We're friends?"

He lifted a shoulder. "Well…you're a case—one I intend to solve. So until then, we're going to stick close together." He didn't repeat the deeper truth: until whoever had left her for dead was caught, she was still in danger. And he wasn't about to leave her vulnerable to another attack if he could help it.

A single tear rolled down her cheek, and he swiped it aside with his thumb.

"What about the baby I was holding?" She pulled her hand from his and wrapped her arms around her stomach as if protecting an unborn child.

Except she'd never carried one. Right? The doctor had

confirmed it. Was the motion just a natural feminine reaction? Or was there something more that he didn't know?

Swallowing the urge to pull her into his arms and promise to hold her until this whole scenario began to make sense, he only offered a gentle smile. "Our first step is figuring out who you are. Once we identify you, we'll find your friends and family. Then maybe one of them can tell us who the baby is and how it ended up with you."

Her nod was slow, thoughtful and sad. "I wish I could do more. I just feel so…so…"

Helpless. He knew the feeling. And the fear of saying it aloud.

But he saw it in the hunch of her shoulders and the silver streaks running down her face. There was just nothing he could do to fix her.

"I'll keep looking. I'll keep asking. I promise. I'm scouring the neighborhood where you were caught on camera. I think I've talked to every busboy, hostess and bartender in a ten-block radius. No leads yet, but I'm not giving up on you."

"But how are we going to figure out who I am if no one remembers me?"

As he scratched his chin, a nurse in blue scrubs clambered into the room, trailed by her rolling electronic work station.

"I'm not quite sure of that. But we'll keep working on it," he said. "Together."

"Good news," the nurse announced. "I think we're going to be able to release you from the ICU today. You're healing right up."

"But what about my mem-memory?" Julie's eyebrows knit together so tight they formed a single line.

The nurse tapped on the keyboard of her laptop on the

rolling stand. "The doctor hasn't said anything new about that. But you're right on schedule."

His heart leaped. Maybe they would know everything soon. "On schedule?"

"Yes, your physical injuries are healing right in the normal range."

He glanced at Julie, whose face shone with the same hope he felt. "And her amnesia?"

"Oh, there's no time line for recovery from amnesia."

"You sure you've never seen this girl?" Zach stabbed a hand through his hair and stopped just long enough to tug on it. Maybe if he pulled it out, he wouldn't spend every day thinking and every night dreaming about how he was going to solve this case. "It was five nights ago around ten o'clock."

In the dim light cascading over glass bottles behind him, the bartender held Julie's picture to his nose. "Nope. I remember all the pretty faces. I'd definitely have remembered her."

That wasn't in doubt. With big brown eyes, a kind smile and porcelain skin, Zach didn't need to ask if she was pretty. He just needed a name. "What if her hair was a little longer? Like this." He held out the digitally modified image of Julie—the one the visual guys at the department had altered by touching up her black eye and giving her long hair again.

"Nope." The barkeep handed the image back across the wooden slab and set back to work with his cleaning cloth. "She missing or something?"

"Yeah. Something like that." Zach tipped his head, pocketing the photos into the front of his jacket. "Thanks for your time."

The bartender, wearing the unstated uniform, tugged at

the collar of his tight black T-shirt. "Want me to keep an eye out for her?"

Turning toward the front door, Zach shook his head. "No, thanks."

He knew where she was. Just not who she was.

The sign above the door read Secrets in big red letters, outlined with small white bulbs. Well, if Julie had been there, then the bar was certainly living up to its name. Whatever secrets this block held, it wasn't eager to give them up. This was his fourth stop in an hour, and no one had recognized either of the pictures.

Sunlight reflected off a passing car, and he squinted against its surprising brilliance. After being in dank bars for longer than he wanted, Zach sucked in the crisp air and warmth of the sun.

There was only one more window front lining the block, its front entrance comprised of twelve rectangular panes set into the green wooden door. With clovers stenciled around the threshold and bay windows, it could be nothing but a traditional Irish pub.

At his wrist a bell jangled on the door handle as he stepped inside.

"We're not open yet." A woman with a long black braid stood at the wooden podium adjacent to the door. As she stuffed paper menus into black leather holders, she followed his motions with eyes nearly as dark as her hair.

Zach grabbed the badge that hung on the chain around his neck and held it out toward her. "Detective Jones with the Minneapolis P.D."

Leaning her elbows on her hostess stand and planting her chin on stacked hands, she blinked up at him. "Civilian Wendy Caruthers. What can I do for you, Officer?"

There was something about the breathy quality of her words, the tilt of her grin. If his brothers had been there, they would have jabbed him in the side and mimicked her tone. His sister, Samantha, would have just laughed at him and told him to ask her out. But since he was alone, he could pretend that he hadn't noticed she was flirting with him.

Or maybe he could leverage it to get the answers he needed.

He quirked the corner of his mouth to match hers. "I'm looking for someone who might have been in here last Friday night. Any chance you were working?"

"I was at the bar the whole night." She tipped her head toward the row of stools in front of a long wooden slab. It was empty now, but in a few hours, it would be crushed with bodies pressing in, looking for something that couldn't be found in the bottom of any bottle. "Who you looking for?"

Reaching into the pocket in the front of his jacket, he produced both pictures, holding them steady under her careful gaze.

"I don't recognize her, but that doesn't mean she wasn't here. We had a rush on Friday after the hockey game let out."

At least she'd recognized Julie as the same person in both pictures. Several of the men on the block hadn't been able to manage that.

"Are you sure? She might have had a baby with her."

A frown marred the woman's attractive face. "Melinda, our hostess, said something about a girl with a kid. On Friday night?"

His heart beat in a crescendo, harder and louder with every second. "Yes. Friday night. Sometime around ten or maybe just before. Can I talk with her?"

"Oh." Wendy's frown deepened. "Melinda's out of the country right now. She's on her honeymoon."

Zach's shoulders fell as a sigh escaped. "Did she say anything at all to you about the girl who was here with a baby? Would Melinda have talked to someone else? Was there anyone else working the front door? A bouncer maybe?"

Wendy swept her gaze over the empty tables lining the dining area, past the small stage and single stool on it. "I don't think so. She was alone all night and keeps to herself mostly, but she'll be back next Tuesday."

"All right. Have her call me as soon as she gets back?" He held out his card, and she took it, brushing her fingers against his as she smiled. That was definitely flirting.

Lots of girls found the badge and gun appealing. But it took the right kind of woman to be with a homicide detective.

And he hadn't come close to finding one of those in the past few years.

Anyway, all he wanted to do was get back to the hospital. Get back to Julie.

Thanking Wendy for her help, he pushed open the door and stepped back into the warm rays of the afternoon sun. It wasn't exactly an immediate break in the case, but maybe it would lead to something to identify Julie.

"According to your chart, you're healing just like I would hope."

Julie pulled her robe closed under her chin and tried to smile at Doctor Willow, who had taken over her care just the day before. "That's good. I guess." Right? She wanted to be healed. She wanted the bruising on her eye to disappear completely, the scratches to fade and her sprained wrist to function normally again.

But more than any of that, she wanted to remember.

His eyes nearly disappeared among the wrinkles as he squinted. "Physically you're in good shape. Your body is doing just what it should. But your mind…" His voice trailed off. "There's nothing I can do to help your memory return more quickly."

"Nothing?" Even if there wasn't a magic pill, there had to be something. "Aren't there exercises? Something I could do to make my brain think in a different way? Like physical therapy for the mind?" She hated the desperation in her voice. It made her sound weak. But she was desperate.

It wasn't just a nuisance. A baby needed her to remember. And she couldn't.

He leaned a hip against the foot of her bed, crossing long legs clothed in pale blue scrubs. Like a kind father, he patted the blanket covering her feet. Had her own dad stood in a similar position or made a similar gesture? Or did he have salt-and-pepper hair and a thin face like the doctor?

She closed her eyes and willed herself to picture her parents.

Nothing.

"Try not to force it." He patted her toes again. "There's no schedule, no normal with amnesia. Sometimes a familiar location or image can jog a memory. Sometimes not."

The only place she knew about for sure was Webster Park. But was she ready to go back there, to see the place where she'd been attacked?

A chill rushed down her arms, and she whispered, "I'm not even sure where to start."

"I know. And that makes this hard to say."

His words sounded like they'd bounced out the back of a truck and tumbled over a gravel road. The wrinkles in his cheeks seemed somehow deeper than before, and a flicker of concern in his nearly vanished eyes stole her breath. "What?" It was more croak than anything else, and he flipped through the papers in his hands.

"Julie, medically you're okay, and I have to discharge you."

His mouth kept moving, but she could hear only the

high-pitched ringing in her ears. Pressure behind her eyes built and threatened to spill as the truth washed over her.

She had nowhere else to go.

"We'll hold on until tomorrow. I'll have the nurse come in to see about making arrangements." Another pat on her feet and he was gone. And she was as alone as she would be in the morning.

She could do nothing but stare at her clenched hands in her lap. The angle of the shadow through the window shifted, and she could do nothing. Paralyzed by fear and terrified to let the pent-up emotions loose, she waited.

She couldn't pinpoint what exactly she was waiting for. Still she waited.

"Julie?"

A weight on her mattress jerked her out of her trance and she blinked into kind eyes. Familiar eyes. "Zach." The word came out on a breath. He held out his arms, and she fell against his chest, resting her ear against the steady thumping of his heart. She tried to measure her breathing to match its pace, but a sob caught her off guard.

Cupping her shoulders with both hands, he held her away from him and looked at her hard. "What's going on?"

"They're releasing me tomorrow."

His head cocked to the side, his eyes shifting back and forth. "Well, that's good. Right? You're getting better."

"Yes. But with my attacker still out there, I don't have any safe place to go."

Like the sun peeking out from behind a cloud, his smile filled her with warmth, and she tilted her face toward it. "You can come home with me."

SIX

As she followed Zach up the stone-lined front walk to the three-story white house, Julie held her breath. Wind whipped through her oversize scrubs—the only outfit the hospital had been able to provide upon her release—and the weight of someone's gaze pressed into her shoulders.

She glanced behind her toward the quiet residential street, every house on the block boasting similar giant oak trees and weathered sidewalks. A chain-link fence herded the barking dog next door, and an old jalopy rattled around the corner.

But there wasn't anyone else around. At least no one she could see.

Still the feeling that someone was watching her sent chills down her back.

Or maybe it was just the uncertainty of walking into a near stranger's home.

"You okay?" Zach had stopped at the front door, his hand on the knob, but he turned back toward her.

She nodded. Then immediately shook her head. "I don't know. Something just feels…"

He abandoned the door and bounded down the two cement steps, coming to a stop right in front of her. "I know. This must be scary, but I promise that you'll really like my sister and brothers. They're cops, too, so you'll be safe until we can solve your case."

He'd made the same argument the night before. But he didn't really have to convince her. Without him, she'd have ended up staying with strangers, completely unprotected, and that was about as appealing as another crack on her head. Anyway, without a real home how could she possibly help him locate the baby she'd been carrying? Yet that didn't change the fact that she barely knew Zach and hadn't met any of his siblings, who shared his home.

"We've got lots of room." He waved at the second-story windows under matching blue gables. "And with you close by, I'll be able to help you look for familiar places that might jump-start your memory."

She nodded again. "Thank you. I don't know where I'd go without you."

The corners of his eyes crinkled, a dimple appearing in his right cheek. "You're safe here. And you're welcome as long as you need a place to crash."

How long would that be? How long would they have to look for her attacker? Or would he come looking for her a third time?

A knot in her stomach clenched at just the thought. Pressing the pad of her finger to the corner of the nearly healed cut on her forehead, she cringed. Next time she might not be so lucky. Next time she could lose a lot more than her memory.

"Come on in." Zach tipped his head back toward the front door. "Let's get you settled."

She rubbed her hands down the front of her pants. She didn't have much of a choice here. Her attacker had left her with no other option, so she put one foot in front of the other, following Zach into the house. As she stepped over the threshold, the weight of someone following her every move melted away.

But that easing tension was replaced immediately by the sheer blast of noise coming from the back of the house. Outside had been all rustling leaves and car engines. Inside was like a football stadium filled with rowdy fans.

"Get that dog out of the kitchen!"

"Not my dog."

The mutt in question barked and yelped before scampering down the wood floors of the hallway, barreling right toward them.

Zach pushed Julie behind him, dropping to a knee to catch the yellow dog in a warm embrace, scratching behind his ears and accepting a lick on his cheek.

"Good boy." Zach ruffled honey-colored fur before looking up at her. "This is Gizmo. He needed a place to stay."

The last word remained unspoken, but it nearly rang in her ears. *Too.* Was he in the habit of bringing home strays? Is that what she was to him? Ears ringing, she managed a smile and patted the dog's head, its coat warm and silky.

"That you, Zach?" A female voice carried down the hall, filling the entryway and probably all the way up the wooden staircase to Julie's left.

"Yes." His call wasn't quite so loud, but traveled just as far. He stood and walked down the hall, motioning for her to follow.

Gizmo trotted at her side, his tongue hanging out of his mouth with every pant. They passed several closed doors before the hallway emptied out into a newly refurbished kitchen, which featured oak cabinets, stainless-steel appliances and a breakfast nook. A tall woman with a short, dark ponytail stood at the stove, while two men with Zach's features lounged at the table, reading the newspaper.

One looked up and caught her eye, which sent heat rising up her neck. The one who made eye contact kicked his brother, who jerked up and surveyed her with a careful gaze, as well. Leaning against Gizmo, who came up almost to her hip, she stared at Zach until he cleared his throat.

"Julie, this is Reese." He pointed at the brother who had been kicked. "And that's Keaton." The kicker. "And that's my little sister, Samantha." The young woman at the stove stopped stirring whatever was in the pot and strolled across the room. Grabbing Julie's hand, she shook it.

"It's good to finally meet you. This guy's been talking about you for ages."

More heat burned her cheeks. She refused to seriously consider what Zach had told them.

"Thank you for letting me stay here."

"What?" Keaton sat up straighter. "Who said anything about you staying here?"

The bottom dropped out of her stomach, and she pressed her hands over it in a vain attempt to keep from crumbling all the way to the floor. Maybe she'd misunderstood. Maybe she really was going to be left to protect herself.

She couldn't tear her gaze away from Keaton, whose eyes squinted very much like Zach's. He ran a hand through his wavy brown hair and tossed his bangs across his forehead. The weight of his stare on the remaining bruises on her face stole her breath, and she reached to run her hand down Gizmo's back. Any connection might help her stand her ground against the unwavering eyes.

But she missed the dog and instead found her fingers tangled with strong, tan ones that gripped her back. Her gaze flowed from their connection all the way up Zach's arm, and she made eye contact. He winked slowly, followed by a gentle squeeze of her hand.

Suddenly her stomach was back in place but filled with a butterfly swarm big enough to match a monarch migration.

And just like those butterflies, an orange oven mitt sailed across the kitchen, smacking Keaton squarely in the chest.

"Quit being a jerk." Samantha's hands pressed into her hips, and her glare silenced the guffaws coming from Reese and the snickers behind Keaton's hand. There was no doubt who ruled the roost inside this home. "She's had a rough week, so be nice."

Julie offered an appreciative smile when Samantha turned back to her.

"Just ignore him. Zach told us all about it last night." Samantha caught the glove that her brother tossed back to her. "I'm sorry to hear about your troubles, but you're welcome here as long as you need a place to stay. And if you need some help shopping or getting a haircut, let me know."

Her hand flew to her uneven locks. She'd done her best to style the sheared mess, but clearly the nurses at the hospital weren't professional stylists. "Thank you. I— That would be great."

Reese resumed his laughter and managed between deep breaths to offer his own greeting. "We're just happy Zach brought you. When he said he was bringing a case home, we thought maybe Homicide had finally cracked him and the morgue was full."

"Homicide?" It conjured images of gory crime scenes and sheet-covered bodies. But the pictures were fuzzy. Pixelated. They weren't real memories. They were…television shows. Crime shows.

Had she watched a lot of TV drama?

Strange that she couldn't remember her name, but she remembered watching shows about crime and punishment.

Or maybe she could remember her name?

Squeezing her eyes closed, she tried to bring her name forward. Tried to force it out of the black.

Nothing.

Maybe her memories were too afraid to show themselves.

"Are you all right?" Zach tugged on her arm. "Let me show you your room."

He slipped back down the hall, his hand resting on the small of her back, guiding her movements. They traipsed up the stairs and down another hallway. Where she thought there should be pictures of the Jones siblings as children, there were pictures of dogs and cats and even a turtle. Each image caught the animal at its most playful, most joyful moment. She could almost feel the breeze in a frame as a giant mutt leaped for a Frisbee, ruffling the dog's fur and turning her cheeks pink.

"These are beautiful."

He didn't even glance at the images as he flipped on a light. "Thanks."

Something about the tone of his voice gave her pause, and she stared at the pictures more closely. "Did you take— Are these yours?"

He laughed, his hands shoved into the depths of his jean pockets. "Don't sound so surprised."

"I'm not. I just didn't realize." She flipped a hand over her shoulder. "They're good. Really."

Like fall leaves rustling down a street and collecting compatriots, his low chuckle grew. "I believe you. Really."

Heat touched her cheeks again, and she slapped her palms against her face. How long had she had this ridiculous blush at the drop of a hat?

Taking pity on her, he leaned a shoulder against a nearby doorjamb and pointed to the image of a green turtle in a white frame on the far wall. "That was my first. My mom signed me up for a photography class the summer I was twelve. I had a broken leg and couldn't take swimming lessons or play in the Little League, but I was driving her crazy holed up in the house. She found this program for kids, and I wasn't too bad at it."

"You're being modest." And he was. The movement and emotion caught in the still images were unlike anything she'd ever seen. At least she couldn't remember seeing anything like that before.

He shrugged it off and pointed a thumb over his shoulder. "This is the guest room. There are clean towels in the closet. I made up the bed with fresh sheets last night. And I put a couple clean T-shirts in the dresser." He opened the top drawer in the solid wood cabinet next to the door. "They'll be too big, but Samantha will help you find some things tomorrow."

She stared at the brown carpet between her feet. "That's really nice of her, but I don't have any money for new clothes."

"I have a few bucks saved up."

Her chin popped up. Was this near-stranger actually offering to buy her something to wear? He was convinced that she was a good investment. But how could he be so sure?

A glint of a smile flickered in the rich chocolate of his eyes. "Just try not to spend all of my money, okay?"

She nodded slowly, emotion choking out any words.

Whether he saw the quiver of her chin or the redness in her eyes, he quickly changed the subject, gesturing toward the guest bathroom across the hall. Samantha's room was right next door, and Reese and Keaton shared a mini-apartment up another flight of wooden stairs. He opened the door to show her, and it creaked loud and eerie.

"What are you showing her up there, Zach?"

The thunderous voice filled every nook and crevice of the house and shot her blood pressure up at least one floor.

"You'll always know if someone is leaving the attic."

Good to know. How had he thought to tell her something like that? So simple, but an easy way to know if one of his brothers was on the second floor. And she didn't have to fear that hideous creaking.

"Which one is your room?"

He pointed toward his feet. "Basement."

"There's another floor? How big is this house?"

He smirked. "Big enough that we don't have to spend all of our time together."

"But you seem to love your family."

"Oh, I do. But you can only take so much of a good thing."

She joined his chuckle, but something shimmied up her spine. It wasn't a memory exactly. Just a feeling. A nudge. "I think I miss my family."

His laughter stopped, and the muscles in his neck tensed. "Do you know who they are?"

"No. I just know I miss them."

The corner of his lips quirked into a crooked grin. "Well, I've never been able to get away from my family long enough to miss them." Pointing his chin toward the frames lining the walls, he continued, "These give me a good excuse to hole up in my darkroom without having to talk to anyone. Sometimes what I need most is something quiet and beautiful after all the ugly I see in Homicide."

Homicide. His brother had said that before.

Her breath caught in her chest, a band around her lungs preventing her from finding more air. Whether from the lack of oxygen or the sudden realization, her head spun. And as he stepped around her, heading down the stairs, she brushed his arm.

"You work Homicide," she wheezed.

"Yes. For a few years now. Why?"

"Why'd you come to my crime scene?"

His face fell, all humor washed away along with the color. His eyes shifted back and forth and finally settled on the painting behind her. Two vertical lines formed between his eyebrows, and his lips pulled into a hard line. "I was close by when the call came over the radio."

That couldn't be the whole truth, so she leaned in a little closer, trying to read the real story in the light reflecting from his eyes. Whatever he wasn't telling her made her stomach roll and her chest burn. What if he hadn't been honest with her? What if they'd known each other before the attack? What if he'd been there with her in the park that night? Heaven forbid, what if he'd been her attacker?

"Tell me what's going on." Fire licked in her belly, rising with an ire built on the uncertainty of her entire existence up until six days before. "The truth can't be any worse than what I'm thinking right now."

The only person she'd thought she could trust wasn't being honest with her, and while her mind couldn't conjure real memories, it had no problem manufacturing horrible scenarios.

Maybe he'd taken on her case to stay close to her, to follow her progression. Maybe he knew she'd seen—and might one day remember—that he'd been in Webster Park that night. Maybe he'd been wielding the wrench or pipe that had left her alone and afraid and looking for someone to trust.

God save her if she'd just made the worst mistake of her life, for there was certainly no one else who would.

Silence hung over them, pregnant with expectation. But he only shoved his hands a little farther into his pockets, before running his hand over his hair, sending the strands shooting in every direction.

As he looked away, her hands began to shake, her heart

beating so hard that it rang in her ears. She had to get out of there. She had to go…somewhere else.

Anywhere else.

She never should have agreed to move into Zach's spare room. And she sure shouldn't have let herself trust him.

Scampering for the top of the stairs, she grabbed the handrail just as Zach wrapped a hand around her elbow. "Wait. I'm sorry. I didn't want to tell you. I didn't think it would help you to know."

Restrained from dashing for the front door, she glared at him over her shoulder. When she jerked her arm away, he let go without a fight.

She'd expected more from a man who would attack a woman. Maybe…

Maybe she'd jumped to conclusions.

Pain washed over his face, and he scrubbed his palms down his cheeks before forcing them back down to his sides. "I'm sorry." His eyes focused on her face. "When I got the call, I was only a couple blocks away. So I was the first on the scene. And I thought you were going to be a dead body."

Her knees gave out, and she sank onto the steps. Everything turned blurry, and she could do nothing but wrap her arms around her knees and bury her face.

Zach dropped down two steps below her, clearly sensing that she needed some space. "I didn't think it would help your recovery to know that when I first saw you, I thought you *were* dead."

It didn't.

And in a small way it did.

How was that possible? How could she have it both ways? She'd known that her attacker had left her for dead. She just hadn't realized how close he'd come to getting what he wanted.

But at least it explained why a homicide detective had been the first to find her—why Zach had taken such an interest in her case.

"I think I need to be alone for a bit."

He patted the toe of her rubber shoe—another hospital donation. "I know this isn't easy for you, but you're not alone."

Zach had promised that they'd work together, that he'd keep her safe.

And he was the only person stepping up to help her. He'd yet to show her any evidence that he couldn't be trusted. And until he did, did she have another choice?

As he loped down the stairs and disappeared around the corner toward the low hum coming from the kitchen, the swirling concoctions in her mind flittered away. Pressing hands over her face, she sent up a weak, disjointed prayer for some sort of understanding and sense of security. Talking to God felt like something she'd done a million times. It also felt foreign, like she hadn't prayed in months. Could she have it both ways?

It didn't matter. Hope that God was listening was all she had to cling to.

God, please let me be safe with him.

"Your hair looks great."

At Samantha's compliment Julie ran her fingers through her much improved pixie cut. Flipping down the visor as they pulled out of the strip mall's parking lot, she tugged at the short ends that hugged her face and framed her eyes.

"That cut is much better than the last one."

Julie managed a smile in response to Samantha's teasing tone. It sure was. After a professional had trimmed it, smoothing out the imbalanced cropping she'd received at the hospital, she looked almost pretty.

Their stop at the department store's cosmetics counter had helped, too. Some concealer covered the remnants of her black and bruised eye, and foundation had smoothed away the remaining imperfections from her attack. A touch of pink to her cheeks and a dash of mascara and she felt just about normal.

Whatever that was.

"Thank you. I feel more like myself. I think." As she flipped the mirror closed, she caught a glimpse of a motorcycle weaving between the cars behind them. Something about the way he maneuvered so recklessly made the snipped hairs on the back of her neck stand on end.

Peeking over her shoulder as Samantha stopped the car at a red light, Julie tried to find him again, but all she could see was the driver's arm three vehicles behind them.

As they idled, Samantha asked, "Something wrong?"

Julie waved her hand. "No. I'm just being silly. It's nothing."

"Nothing, like we should hit the next store? Or nothing, like I should call Zach?"

The row of shopping bags filling the backseat rustled as they took off. New jeans and tops, shoes and scarves. Everything she could possibly need to start over.

"Oh, don't bother your brother. I just saw a motorcycle rider who was kind of aggressive." She shook off the strange tension in her middle. "I'm sure everything is all right."

Samantha nodded slowly, her gaze flicking toward her mirror. "I saw him, too."

Of course she had. Samantha was a police officer, just like her brothers. She'd definitely notice someone out of place or if something should cause concern. But she sat with a relaxed posture, her wrist draped across the steering wheel.

If she wasn't worried, Julie had no reason to be, either.

Another glance behind her, and the rider on his sporty bike had vanished.

See? Nothing to worry about.

Letting out a slow breath, she turned back to Samantha. "Thank you for spending your day off shopping with me."

"I'm happy to, but you should thank Zach. He's the one who sponsored this spree." A wicked grin made her brown eyes—so much like Zach's—sparkle. "He just doesn't know that he bought me a few things while we were at it."

Julie laughed aloud, running her hands down her pant leg. "I don't understand why he's been so generous."

"Even when we were kids, he'd bring home lost and sick animals. Gizmo is just the most recent in a string of pets needing a home."

"Are those the cats and dogs in the pictures?"

Samantha nodded. "Zach's a good guy, and he can't turn his back on a stray in need."

Her words—though not intentionally cruel—punched Julie in the gut.

A stray in need.

Could there be a more apt description? He saw her as just another stray needing a temporary home.

Why did that realization make her lungs have to fight for air when just the night before she'd fallen asleep in his guest bed wondering if she could truly trust him? Maybe her amnesia was making her crazy.

Tires behind them squealed, and both women jumped, instantly alert. Twisting in her seat, Julie tried to find the source of the commotion, but the cars behind their two-door coupe were pulling into a line at another light.

All except for the motorcycle.

The driver in all black, his face obscured by a full helmet, revved his engine, shooting down the double yellow line toward them.

"What is he doing?"

"I don't know, but let's get out of here." Samantha cranked the wheel and slammed her foot against the pedal, steering through a fishtail and down a small side road.

Julie couldn't tell if the sound of her heartbeat was louder than the car's engine, but all she could hear was the progressive thumping. Faster and faster as they picked up speed and as the motorcycle gained on them.

"Call Zach. Tell him what's going on, and that we need him to get over here." Samantha had morphed from easygoing shopping companion to cop in two beats.

With shaking fingers, Julie stabbed at the numbers on her phone but turned back to Samantha before completing the call. "Where are we? Where do I tell him to find us?"

"We're headed on County Road 33 toward the Winchester Bridge."

Julie nodded just as Zach answered, but the roaring in her ears rose above his voice and the growling engine. Without waiting for him to ask why she had called, she plunged in. "I'm with Samantha. We're being followed by a guy on a motorcycle, and he's trying to run us off the road."

For a split second she thought that her heartbeats had rendered her temporarily deaf. And then his eerily calm voice split the silence. "Where are you?" She relayed the directions Samantha had given her. "I'm not far away. I can be there in ten minutes. And I'll call in for backup. Hang on until someone gets there. This is going to be okay."

Oh, how she wanted to believe him. "We'll try."

The car veered sharply, and her shoulder slammed against the window, the phone flying from her hand as they sailed past towering pine trees. The motorcycle drew even with their back bumper. Samantha swerved again, but the cycle matched her movements, dodging a connection that would have sent him into the ditch. He skidded around a blue sign announcing the upcoming lake but was immediately on their tail again.

And in her side mirror, Julie couldn't miss the handgun the rider brandished.

Too afraid that she'd distract Samantha, Julie didn't say a word. She clenched her door, offering up soundless prayers for protection over and over again. All the time unable to rip her eyes from the gun in the hands of their pursuer.

When the barrel leveled, she tried to alert Samantha, who continued to push the little car to its limits, but her warning vanished beneath the crack of a gunshot as her window shattered.

SEVEN

Julie screamed in time with the second gunshot, which blew out the tire beneath her feet.

The car swerved across the center line of the two-lane highway, but Samantha managed to keep it out of the ditch with a white-knuckled grip.

Refusing to turn around enough to see if the motorcyclist was still on their tail, Julie clamped her mouth closed and stared at the ceiling. God had to save them, for no one else could at this point.

"Hang on!" Samantha's cry seemed to light the tension in the car until it sparked and crackled, burning away all the oxygen in the vicinity.

A horn blew long and low from down the road, and two dark headlights on either side of an eighteen wheeler's grill bore down on them. The driver behind the wheel flashed his lights, but the car's response was sluggish at best.

God have mercy.

Please have mercy.

She could do little more than repeat the mantra in her head and fight for every tiny breath against the fear that squeezed her chest and threatened to steal her sanity.

Someone had already filched her mind, and now he was about to take the rest of her, too. And all she could see was the trucker's face—his eyes wide and mouth nearly unhinged. The wispy blond beard was straight out of the eighties, as it hung over his plaid shirt. Terror filled every crevice of his craggy face not covered by his beard, and he rocked like he was pumping the brakes as hard as he could.

It wasn't going to work. And even from fifty feet away, she could see that he knew it, too. She'd remember that face for the rest of her life. However long that was.

And then the little coupe, which had been in place to be T-boned on the passenger side, shook. The engine screeched, protesting the hand brake that Samantha yanked.

"Hang—"

That was all that Samantha could get out before the car lurched, suddenly flying. And spinning off the road.

Julie's seat belt jerked across her chest, rubbing her neck raw.

Dizzy from tumbling down the embankment, she prayed that the car would stop rolling, and it did. With a sickening splash.

Immediately her stomach followed the sinking motion of the coupe as water covered the floorboards. The recently frozen lake water made her feet tingle, already dragging down the hem of her jeans.

They had to get out of the car or be trapped in the frigid water.

But Samantha wasn't moving.

Zach threw his car into Park at the top of the hill, hanging up with the emergency dispatcher and racing down the uneven tracks left by Samantha's car, which he'd seen careen off the road, thankfully unscathed by the tractor trailer. Throwing off his jacket and tie at the water's edge, he tossed them in a pile with his phone and badge before jumping into the churning mess.

The coupe was still halfway above water, resting on the lake's bottom before what was certainly a steep drop-off. But he couldn't see through the shattered passenger window to his sister. To Julie.

Running through water in his jeans was a practice in frustration, the sodden material leaving him sluggish and breathless. Or maybe that was the freezing water, sucking the life out of him.

But at least he was still moving. Julie and Samantha weren't making any visible progress out of the car. Pressing hard, he paddled with his hands through the brown murkiness. It seemed to take three years with lungs burning to cross the ten yards. Finally the icy door handle was in his grip, just below the surface of the water.

He yanked on it. It didn't budge.

He twisted over the hood of the car and leaned in close to the windshield. The sun's reflection caught his eye, and he winced away before cupping his hands around his face and peering into the darkness.

Then he saw her. Julie writhed and clawed at Samantha's belt buckle, which was nearly submerged by the water inside. His sister's head lolled to the side, a dark streak running from the edge of her hairline across her forehead.

He had to get in there. He had to get them to safety.

When he pounded on the windshield, Julie jumped, her eyes wild when she saw him. Then she mouthed his name. Or maybe she screamed it, but the only sound in his ears was like rushing water.

"Open the door." He pointed at it, but she shook her head, her lips forming another word.

Stuck.

The water pressure held it firmly in place, but he had to get them out before the water rose any higher.

Shooting a glance up at the lonely stretch of highway, he wished his sister's favorite hair person lived closer to the center of the city instead of on the outskirts. But she didn't, and they'd ended up at the base of this nearly abandoned bridge.

Then again, at least he'd been nearby when Julie had called. That seemed to be a trend with her.

Help was still a long way out, and he had to do something now.

Giving the door handle another vain attempt, he slogged around to the rear of the hatchback, which wasn't submerged.

Relief made his hands and feet tingle.

Back at the windshield, he slapped the glass in rapid succession until Julie looked back at him. With stilted movements, he pointed at the rear door, then mimed crawling over the seat and unlatching it.

She shook her head and pointed at Samantha.

He'd take care of his sister. He would. But first, he had to get into the car.

"Trust me." He poked himself in the chest and repeated the inaudible words.

Squinting at him, she tugged on her lower lip. Her hesitation was colder than the lake. Did she not trust him?

Finally she nodded, squirming toward the rear. He raced to meet her at the back, and when the latch clicked, he threw it open, grabbing her hands and pulling her into the waist-deep water.

"Are you hurt?"

"No." She shook her head hard and then flung her hands toward his sister. "Samantha won't wake up. I think she hit her head on the steering wheel. And I couldn't get her unbuckled."

As he pulled a knife from his pocket, he said, "Can you make it to shore? Wait for me there."

Again, she paused. Again, the truth of her suspicion needled in the depth of his stomach.

"All right." She plashed away.

He watched her struggle up the moderate incline for a split second before sliding into the back of the car. Squashing shopping bags as he went, he used his elbows to pull himself toward the steering wheel. He reached over the black leather seat and, as his hand wrapped around the seat belt buckle, another hand pushed his away.

His gaze flew up to meet his sister's.

"I've got it." Her chest rose and fell with loud, labored breaths, but she freed herself and followed him out of the car, grabbing the shopping bags as they fell back into the water.

He pulled the bags out of her hands and wrapped an arm around her waist, nearly carrying her to the shore. He wasn't fast enough for Julie, who ran to meet them in the knee-deep water.

She hugged Samantha's other side, bearing much of the weight of the larger, stumbling woman. "I am so sorry." The words nearly vanished, carried away by a brisk wind.

Before he could ask what she meant, the sirens arrived and with them help in every form. Blue uniforms swarmed the scene, settling Samantha onto a stretcher and asking a hundred questions a minute.

Zach had never been on this side of the inquisition, and he found that all he really wanted to do was make sure that Samantha was okay, that his case hadn't cost him more than he could bear to lose. And then he wanted to hold Julie close and whisper assurances that this wasn't her fault. That she was safe.

That he'd find the man responsible for threatening her and see justice done.

A medic wrapped a blanket around Julie's shoulders, but she continued to shiver as she answered every question thrown at her. Zach pulled off the wrap he'd been given and layered it on her back. She looked his way, and he offered a silent nod of encouragement.

She was doing great. An old pro at responding to all of the questions.

He just hated that she had to be.

"There was a man on a motorcycle. He was following us, and Samantha tried to lose him." She glanced toward the once empty pavement, which was now dotted with two ambulances, three squad cars and his unmarked sedan. "But he was on one of those really fast racing bikes, and he caught up to us in no time at all."

"Did you get a plate number or a make of the motorcycle?" The officer chewed on the end of his pen, holding it poised against his notepad.

"No. It had neon green on it, and I might recognize it if I saw a picture of it, but it all happened so fast."

The uniform scribbled into his pad, but Zach could only watch Julie's face. Her jaw shifted back and forth, a visible account of the tension that overtook her and her fight to release it. She'd either conquered her tears or found that grinding her teeth was a better outlet.

But her telltale hands never lied. Holding her blanket closed below her chin, they trembled.

He couldn't take this experience away. He couldn't turn back time or pretend that everything was going to be all right.

So he did the only thing he could do. He slipped an arm around her back.

Every muscle in her tensed for a moment before she relaxed and fell into his side.

The questioning cop shot Zach a curious look that stopped at the badge hanging on the chain around his neck. "I don't suppose you saw his face?"

"No. He had a full black helmet on." Sidling closer to Zach, she squeezed her eyes closed. "About half a mile back he pulled a handgun and shot at my window. It shattered, and I couldn't see much else from then on."

She sounded so cool about the whole thing, her voice steady. So why was his grip around her waist tightening? He'd nearly lost his case—his only lead on the missing baby.

At least that's the answer he was going to give himself.

"But I know I heard another shot, and that's when the tire blew, and we crossed the center line." Her whole body shivered.

"All right. We'll want to get you into the station to see if you can identify the bike."

"I'll make sure she comes in this afternoon." Zach hadn't said anything else, but he had to do something to make her stop quivering, and the only thing he knew to do was to take charge.

The uniform nodded, tipped his head and walked away. Despite the hubbub of slamming doors and an ambulance roaring to life, it felt like they were all alone in the world.

He turned her toward him, running his palms up and down her arms.

"Are you okay?"

She bit her bottom lip and offered a half nod, half shake

of her head. "The paramedic said that I'm not injured. I'll probably be a little stiff, but I'll be fine."

He dipped at the knees until their eyes were on the same level. "I didn't ask if you were hurt, I asked if you're okay. Are you holding it together?"

"I'm— It's going to—" The shaking in her hands returned, fluttering her blanket. "I'm just a little shaken up. I'll be okay."

She was brave. Braver than he'd have been in the same situation. Braver than he was at the moment, when all he wanted to do was take her some place where she'd never be in danger again.

That just wasn't an option.

No place was safe until they solved her case.

"All right. We're going to go to the station and take a look at some motorcycle models to see if you can identify the one the guy who shot at you was riding. After that we're going to go home and get your new clothes cleaned up." He nudged the pile of soggy bags with his toe. Count on Samantha—even after a car crash—to rescue new clothes. "Then what would you like to do?"

She paused, the lines around her mouth disappearing as fear ebbed away like the gentle waves on the lakeshore. "I just want to go some place peaceful. Some place I don't have to be afraid."

He gave her elbow a gentle squeeze. "Can you give me a little more direction than that?"

She glanced toward the heavens, puffy white clouds floating across the blue sky like a cathedral. A slow curve of her pink lips replaced the thin line of anxiety that had held that position.

In her previous life, had she stood under a sky so perfect, so secure? Was there a memory locked deep inside under the same sun?

He couldn't risk asking.

Because her answer would upset her even more. She didn't know the truth any more than he did.

"I want to go to church."

It wasn't as though Julie cognitively recognized the building or the people, but something about Zach's little community church was familiar. Maybe it was the way the older woman at the front door shook her hand and smiled. Or perhaps it was the gentle melody drifting from the baby grand at the front of the room.

Something felt right about being in church again.

Maybe it had been a while since she'd been inside a church building.

She couldn't be certain, but as she sank into a padded chair, she let the peace and joy in the room settle over her, the weight that had been so heavy on her shoulders finally lifting.

Zach slipped in beside her, resting his arm on the back of her chair. "Is this what you were hoping for?"

"Exactly." Well, almost. She smoothed her sheared locks down and offered a wavering smile. Even if they hadn't told her that they cut her hair at the hospital, she'd have known that this style wasn't her norm.

He followed the movement of her hand, and after a long second, reached up to run his finger from the top of her hair to her temple. "I like your hair like that. It suits you."

Not the most romantic, as far as compliments went. Yet it set her heart fluttering in a brand new way. This wasn't fear or uncertainty. She'd had enough of that lately to know the difference. This was…attraction?

Of course not.

Sitting up straight, she locked her gaze on the front of the sanctuary where a wooden cross hung behind a simple podium. She needed to focus on the cross, not the tingling line that traced the path of his fingers.

She couldn't afford to be distracted by a handsome face. Even if that face had perfect features, a stunning smile and paralyzing brown eyes.

The accident the day before hadn't been an accident at all. It was a warning, a threat. Another attempt on her life. Someone wanted her dead, and that someone might have taken the missing baby. Her hands began to tremble, and she clasped them together in her lap to keep them still.

It didn't help.

They had to do something. They had to find that baby.

Well, Zach had to do something. She was still mostly useless, not even able to identify the motorcycle that had run her and Samantha off the road. And her memories of the night in the park were as locked up as ever.

She pulled away from the warmth of Zach's arm, but he didn't get the hint. He was still looking at her, still leaning in slightly as though waiting for something.

Like her response. "Um…thank you."

"You're quite welcome. I mean it. You look really pretty." He straightened his collar, his usual tie and jacket conspicuously absent, and glanced at his sister. Samantha had insisted on joining them after the E.R. doctor confirmed that she had nothing more than a bump on her head and a few bruises from the car accident. Reese and Keaton had attended Saturday services the night before, as they were both on duty that morning.

And knowing that the laughing brothers were somewhere out there watching over the city helped Julie breathe a little easier.

A rotund man with thinning black hair walked to the front of the stage. "Let's all stand and sing hymn number three forty-two, 'It is Well with My Soul.'"

Pulling the well-loved hymnal from the pocket in the back of the chair in front of them, Zach flipped it open just as the music swelled.

"When peace like a river attendeth my way… When sorrows like sea billows roll…"

Julie closed her eyes, letting the words rise in a melodic prayer. Lifting her face to the ceiling, she promised that no matter her lot, she would say, "It is well with my soul."

Zach's tenor harmony blended with her voice for four verses, and when they sat back down, even the bruise across her throat and chest didn't hurt. This is what she'd missed. But for how long had she been missing it? Had it been weeks or months since she sat in a chair like this? Was it possible she'd turned her back on the thing she needed most?

"You knew all the words to that song." His voice in her ear made her jump. Or maybe it was what he said. A shiver raced down her spine, and she pressed a hand over her mouth.

She'd known the words.

All of them.

My sin, oh, the bliss of this glorious thought!
My sin, not in part but the whole,
Is nailed to the cross, and I bear it no more,
Praise the Lord, praise the Lord, O my soul!

That was the whole third verse, and she knew it. By heart. In her heart.

The lyrics were written there. Unforgotten and true.

Sitting up a little straighter, she let a smile creep into place. Zach offered her a matching grin and a squeeze of her hand as the pastor opened his Bible and set it on the lectern. The microphone crackled as he straightened it out before reading the selected scripture, but Julie didn't hear a word of it.

She remembered.

She remembered!

It was only a start, true. But would the rest come back fast enough to help the missing baby?

At the benediction, Zach stood and led Julie toward the center aisle. He wanted to grab her hand and relive the flip of his stomach at her incandescent smile, but this wasn't the place. And it certainly wasn't the time.

His heart didn't agree.

He just wanted to celebrate with her. The memories she'd longed to unlock had finally begun returning. He couldn't keep silent at that.

The crowd flowed slowly down the row, church members stopping to chat here and there. When they were finally free of the single-file confinement, he stepped aside and encouraged Julie to step up to his side with a hand at the small of her back.

Suddenly her body stiffened and her eyes grew wide, unblinking.

"Julie? What's going on?"

She remained motionless and silent, and he followed the line of her gaze until it landed on a young mother holding an infant wrapped in pink blankets.

"Kay."

"You're good?"

"No. The baby I was carrying. Her name is Kay."

EIGHT

"What did you say?" Zach grabbed for Julie's arm, not quite sure if he was using it to hold himself up or to keep her standing.

Julie didn't turn away from the mom holding her child about fifteen feet away from them. Without blinking and with barely a twitch of her mouth, she whispered, "The baby. The missing baby. The one I was carrying."

Yes, he knew who she was talking about. He needed more. He needed her to repeat the last thing she said.

"Her name is Kay." She spoke in such a nonchalant tone that he had to shake himself alert. This wasn't small potatoes, as his mom would say. This changed everything.

Still Julie didn't move, so he turned to Samantha. "We'll meet you in the parking lot in a moment. We just need a second."

His sister cocked her head to the side, eventually nodding and returning to her route to the foyer. He didn't waste time chatting with anyone else; instead he ushered Julie toward a small alcove off the side of the sanctuary. The little prayer room had emptied, and he guided her to one of the seats that lined the walls. She sank into it, and he dropped to his knees before her. His hands swallowed hers, but he kept his grip gentle, encouraging her to open up.

And then he waited. And he prayed.

Please, let her remember something else. Please, help her to remember. The words became his mantra while she remained transfixed on a distant point over his shoulder. Her jaw worked back and forth, back and forth as her nostrils flared and her hands began to tremble.

"Julie, can you tell me what you remember?"

She blinked once as though surprised to find him before her. Then tears gushed into her doe eyes, spilling down her cheeks and dripping off her chin. Grabbing a tissue from the package on a neighboring chair, he dabbed at the streaks, stroking her cheek with his thumb.

"Lonnie."

What about Kay? he wanted to ask, but Julie began again before he could open his mouth.

"Lonnie couldn't have even been twenty. She was so young. And she was scared. And she asked me to hold Kay. She said she'd be right back. She said she just needed to run an errand and couldn't take her baby with her." Julie's lower lip began to quiver, and she chomped down on it even as her eyebrows pulled together. Lines around her mouth grew deep, something akin to pain flickered in her eyes. "I—I don't think Lonnie came back for her baby. I don't know what happened to he-er."

Her sob ripped at his heart. There was nothing to do but pull her into his arms and whisper a prayer over her. But his words were illogical. They blended together into a mess. Thankfully his God was big enough to make sense of his mutterings.

Julie's sobs shook her body, a damp spot growing in the notch between his neck and shoulder. Her hands fisted into the front of his shirt as he rubbed a figure eight into her back. His heart thudded in his own ears, but she didn't seem to mind its heavy rhythm.

"You're safe now. And we'll figure out what happened to Kay."

It could have been ten seconds or ten minutes that he held her, but eventually she pulled away, sniffing loudly. Without pretense she blew her nose and hiccupped twice before meeting his gaze again.

His arms felt empty. Strange. They hadn't been like that before. Before he'd calmed and soothed her.

"Can you—" He cut himself off, searching for the right phrase to get her talking again. Reminding her that she couldn't remember much else wasn't going to help. "What is it that scared you?"

"I was holding her. I had this baby in my arms, and when Lonnie didn't come back, I didn't—I didn't know what to do. And I was afraid for her. I didn't know what was going to happen to her. All of a sudden I was responsible for this little one, and I—" She held up her hands and shook her head.

He nodded. "I understand." Now to get more information without letting her clam up. He took a deep breath through his nose, letting it out slowly through his mouth. Then again. And a third time until she followed suit. The cleansing breath seemed to clear her eyes. At least they focused on his face instead of the far wall.

"You don't have to be scared anymore."

"But Kay is out there somewhere without her mom."

He nodded, the truth a knife to his gut. "You're right. So let's find her."

"All right. How?"

"What did Lonnie look like? You said she was young. What else?"

Dark lashes fluttered closed, her lips pressed together. "She was wearing a hat. Like a baseball cap, but it was pulled low over her face. And all of her hair was tucked under it. And her scarf was pulled up clear to the tip of her chin. I think it was dark. Her face was shadowed."

Well, that description was going to be about as useful as a fishing line without a hook. Trying to give her a smile that didn't say what he was really thinking, he nodded. "What about baby Kay? What did she look like?"

Julie frowned. "Like a baby."

"Right. But were there any distinguishing characteristics or birthmarks? What color was her hair?"

"Brown, dark." She reached a hand to her cheek, running several fingers over her freckles. "And she had a red mark on her face. Almost square, right here."

Now they were getting somewhere. "A birthmark or a bruise?"

She closed her eyes again. "I think it was a birthmark. It wasn't purple. More like a strawberry mark."

He reached to hug her, but he couldn't risk indicating an end to the interview, so he let his arms drop to rest on her knees. But that seemed too intimate, too familiar. Letting them drop limply at his sides, he said, "Is there anything else? Where did you meet Lonnie?"

Panic flashed across her face. "I don't know."

"Okay, where were you when she gave you the baby to hold?"

The same apprehension, the same response. "I don't know." The tears returned, welling up and splashing down. "Why can't I remember?"

When the urge hit him again, he didn't hesitate to pull her close. "I don't know." He ran a hand over her hair and down the back of her neck. "But it's coming back. At least you're remembering something."

She nodded into his neck, pressing her ear against his traitor heart, which insisted on picking up speed. He held her until she pulled away and stood. Rising slowly after her, he held a hand out toward the door. "Ready to go look for Kay?"

She nodded, gliding out of the room.

In the parking lot they met Samantha, who was leaning against his car, arms crossed over her chest. "What took you guys so…" Her eyes flew wide. "Hey, are you all right?"

"Yeah. Why?" She motioned to his shirt, and he looked down at the wrinkles over his chest and the damp, black marks on his shoulder. "We—We were— We just—"

Julie came to his rescue. "I remembered something."

Samantha's smile outshone the sun as she pulled Julie close. "I am so happy for you, Julie." Pink dotted her cheeks. "Or is it something else?"

"Julie's good for now."

For now.

It wouldn't be much longer before the rest of her memories came back. Until then, he'd follow every lead that she could provide. Whenever she could provide it.

For a Sunday afternoon the police station was awfully busy. Julie dodged the feet of a man in handcuffs slumped in a chair near the front desk. He tipped up his chin and puckered his lips, making a crude gesture. Cringing, she slipped nearer to Zach's side.

Too much closer and they'd be sharing the same coat.

But there was something about the way he'd taken care of her during her meltdown at the church that confirmed her hopes. He was safe. And she was secure with him.

There was also something about the way he'd wrapped his arms around her that had stirred something else. Something that made her stomach flip and her heart race. Not fear. Not uncertainty.

Although she wasn't exactly sure what it was.

It was just…nice.

Zach frowned at the man in cuffs, wrapping an arm around Julie's waist. "Stay close."

Yep. That was nice.

She nodded as they wound their way past the desk sergeant and into a bull pen of desks. Clumped in groups of twos and threes, the metal monstrosities took over the entire room, in some spots leaving barely enough space to squeeze between. Zach just pulled her in a little closer in the tight spots.

When they reached a desk toward the back of the room, he pointed to a chair at its end, while sliding into his own seat. Flipping on the computer monitor, he pulled up a search engine. "This is the missing-persons database for all of Minnesota. Let's see if Lonnie or Kay is listed."

He tapped on his keyboard until a results screen popped up.

She leaned over the edge of the desk, nearly at his shoulder, searching for a picture or something that would jog her memory. Seeing a mom with her baby that morning had been like sticking her finger into a light socket—the memories jolting and jarring. And more than a little bit painful.

More than the images, emotions filled her entire chest, wrapping around her lungs and squeezing her heart. It was like she was experiencing them for the first time, and she hadn't been able to keep herself in check.

"No one by those names is listed." He let out a long sigh.

"Maybe another spelling? Or maybe it was Kate instead of Kay. Maybe I misheard her. Maybe Kay is just a nickname." She hated how desperate she sounded.

He typed a bit more. Another screen popped up. Same result.

Drumming his fingers on the desk, he stared at the ceiling for a long second. "Well, let's search by her birthmark."

Oh, let that be a birthmark.

"What?" His tone dropped.

Had she spoken out loud? "Hmm?"

With squinting eyes he assessed her. "Are you not sure about the birthmark on her cheek?"

"No. I am." Except for the knot in her stomach. She could see it in her mind's eye. But could she believe that image? Her mind had had no trouble fabricating other stories. "It's just, what if my memory is wrong? What if I'm misremembering?"

Spinning his knees toward her, he leaned forward and cupped her folded hands inside his. "Listen to me carefully." He waited until she glanced up to meet his stare, his eyes soft, his lips gently pursed. "You're doing your best. I trust you. I trust that you're giving me everything you can." His grip around her hands tightened as he pressed his palms together, and she welcomed his strength, releasing a pent-up breath. "We're going to check out everything you remember, as soon as you remember it. And when we find something, we'll double-check."

"But what if we're just wasting time?" Why couldn't she just agree with him? Why couldn't she just believe? What was wrong with her?

"We're just going to keep digging. It's the only thing we can do." His voice was soft and firm at the same time. Certain and steadfast. "We're not going to sit back and hope something happens. We're going to look for her. And that starts with finding more of your memories. We'll find Kay and her mom, and we'll find the man who did this to you."

By the time he finished speaking, his elbows were on his knees as he bent all the way over at the waist, and she mirrored his position. A few strands of hair fell across his forehead, and she freed one of her hands to brush it back into place. A warm scent of earthy aftershave followed her hand as she brought it to her throat.

It had been a while since she'd been this close to such an attractive man. She didn't need a distinct memory to be certain of that. She just *knew*.

A smile played at the corners of his lips, his boyish dimple hollowing out his right cheek. "What are you thinking?"

There were no words in her vocabulary to describe her thoughts—or, more accurately, her feelings. She wanted to be near him, to borrow some of his assurance and be swallowed in his strong embrace.

She leaned even farther in toward him. His eyes followed her movement, drawing her closer until there was barely a foot between them.

"Jones!"

Zach jerked up, ramrod straight, and dropped her hands. Pushing with his feet, he pedaled his chair back until he bumped into another desk. "Ramirez!"

Heat shot up her neck and curled around her ears. They'd been caught almost kissing. In the middle of a bustling police station.

Could she be any more stupid? She'd nearly kissed a man she'd only just met.

No matter how kind his smile or gentle his eyes, she had no business thinking of Zach as anything other than the cop working her case. Seriously.

All right, he was a generous cop, who'd given her a place to stay and new clothes. A cop who hadn't hesitated to jump into a freezing lake to rescue her and his sister. A cop with a kind heart, who adopted stray dogs....

Strays. Samantha had told her the truth. Zach rescued strays, and Julie was just another.

She had nothing to offer any man—let alone a distinguished police officer with a family and a home and a life. Until she knew who she was, she had no business letting her mind even wander down those kinds of roads. And when she did remember, well, then she'd be headed back to her home. And to her family.

There were people out there waiting for her, looking for her. She knew it. She just couldn't name them.

Until she found them, almost kissing the man who had given her a temporary home and his protection could only lead to more embarrassment.

Covering her face with her hands, she peeked through her fingers at the officer who had interrupted them. Thank goodness he'd spoken or she'd have made an even bigger fool of herself.

"You got a call from someone at McNulty's Pub. Wendy." Ramirez flipped his pad open, reading from his notes. "She said your girl Melinda called in. She's definitely not going to be stateside until late this week."

Zach's shoulders fell, and he squinted his eyes. "Perfect."

When he looked back at her, it took everything Julie had not to ask who Melinda and Wendy were.

Apparently he could read the question on her face. "McNulty's is near Webster Park, and Wendy thought there might have been a woman with a baby in there on the night you were attacked. I'm just waiting to hear back from the hostess, who is currently on her honeymoon."

"McNulty's." She let the word stroll over her tongue, whispering it several more times. "No. I don't remember it." Ramirez's face fell, so she quickly added, "But that doesn't mean anything. I don't remember much yet."

"You will." Zach shot her a smile, walking his chair back to the front of his desk and picking up his phone. "And until then let's see if anything you remember might help the U.S. Marshals."

Why hadn't she thought of that?

He pulled a card from his desk drawer and punched the number into his phone. "Serena Summers? This is Detective Zach Jones with the—" Marshal Summers must have cut him off, as he stopped short. "Yes. Julie remembered that the baby she was carrying is named Kay and her mother is named Lonnie. Do those names mean anything to you?"

Zach's gaze settled on Julie, the weight tangible, but he didn't say anything. "All right. Let me ask her." Punching the hold button, he set the receiver back into its cradle without shifting his eyes. "They want to talk with you in person and show you a few more pictures."

"I don't remember that guy Frank that they showed me last time."

"They know that, but a baby showed up in Denver around the time that Kay disappeared, and they want to know if she might be the same baby. What do you think?"

The day's emotions and breakthroughs rushed back through her, stealing her strength and depositing it somewhere out of reach. Sinking back against her chair, she offered the only response she could manage, a loose nod.

Picking the phone back up and punching the button, he said, "When can you be here? Tomorrow morning. Good. We'll meet you at the police station at eight-thirty. See you then."

After hanging up, he spun back toward her. "They're hopping a flight first thing tomorrow morning."

"Good." She couldn't muster anything more.

He stood. She stared, unable to match his movements.

"I was going to ask if you wanted to look through another group of mug shots, but you look beat." Taking her hands, he lifted her from the chair until she was close enough to fall into his arms. If she wanted to. Which she did not. Much.

Tilting his head toward the door, he said, "Why don't we get you home to get some rest? Serena and Josh are going to check Lonnie and Kay's names against the national missing-persons database." Tucking her into his side, he moved through the maze. "You've had a pretty big day, huh?"

A yawn caught her off guard as she leaned on his shoulder. Before she could blink, she was back in his car being whisked away to his home. The steady hum of the engine rocked her until she couldn't think of anything but how silly she'd been. First to doubt that Zach was a good man. And then to nearly kiss him.

She wasn't anything special to him, but she was most certainly safe with him.

At least in that moment.

NINE

Zach stared at the face of the clock on the wall as Serena and Josh settled into seats at the table opposite Julie and him. Eight twenty-nine. Right on time. Nodding at each of the marshals, he folded his hands on the table. Either that or he might try to put his arm around Julie again. And that didn't exactly convey professionalism.

"Thank you for meeting with us again." Josh directed his comment to Julie, but offered Zach a nod of greeting.

"Whatever I can do to help find Kay." Julie leaned forward, her eyes bright. Apparently she hadn't been plagued by a sleepless night that had very little to do with a case filled with dead ends and far too much to do with wondering what would have happened in the bull pen if Ramirez hadn't interrupted them.

He scooted his chair another inch away from the woman to his right. More space meant more cognizant thought.

Of course, anything would be an improvement over nearly kissing her the day before. What had he been thinking? Well, he hadn't been thinking. That was the problem. She'd just been so pretty with those big eyes and quivering lip. He'd wanted to comfort her.

And, to some extent, himself.

But this wasn't the time or the place for a romantic attachment. She was a case. And she would leave as soon as it was solved. Not to mention, she had plenty on her plate at the moment. Finding Kay. Unearthing lost memories. Running from a guy trying to kill her.

He had no business working her case and kissing her. She needed his protection. And getting emotionally involved would keep him from giving her his very best.

Glancing at the spot where her hands held on to the edge of the table, Julie took a deep breath. "If I was the last person to see her—to hold her—I'll do whatever I can."

Pulling a small digital recorder from his pocket, Josh set it on the table. "Mind if I record our conversation?"

"Go ahead."

He pressed a button, and a tiny red light cast its shadow across the glossy wooden tabletop.

Serena opened a file, pulling out several large pictures. "We appreciate that. Can you identify any of these people as Lonnie or baby Kay? Let's start with the women."

"Sure." With the tips of her fingers, Julie pulled the pictures across the table, staring into first one face, then another and another. She stretched her neck for a closer look at the fourth image, finally shaking her head. "I don't think so." Shutting her eyes, she took several beats in silence, and Zach wanted nothing more than to hold on to her hand as she ventured back into the veiled recesses of her mind.

"Lonnie's hair was tucked into a hat, and it was dark, but her face was thinner—her cheeks kind of hollow, her eyes scared. And she was just a kid. So young."

"What's your best guess at her age?" Serena poised her pen on the file, ready to take the note.

"Maybe eighteen. Maybe not quite."

After scribbling with her pen, Serena collected the images and tucked them back into place. "Do you have any other memories of her? Do you know where you met or where she went?"

"I don't know. Like I said, it was dark."

Zach bit his tongue to keep from reminding them that the video had a time stamp that set the ordeal somewhere in the neighborhood of ten at night. Maybe it was dark because it was night. But that wasn't worth breaking the flow of Julie's interview.

Trouble filtered across her face, like a light through partially open blinds. "I don't remember anything else about her, but something in here—" she pressed a hand to the blue T-shirt covering her stomach "—tells me that she didn't come back for Kay."

"Do you think this could be the baby you were carrying? Kay?" Josh pushed a single piece of picture paper across the table, and Julie held it at arm's length. It was a small child with fair hair, round cheeks and a toothless grin.

With a slow shake of the head, she said, "It's not her." As she offered it back, she continued, "Kay had dark hair and a birthmark—I think—on her cheek."

Both marshals instantly sat a little taller, a little straighter. Josh's jaw hung slack for a second. "Are you sure it was a birthmark?"

"Well, I mean, it could have been a bruise, but it was more square than that. It was a strawberry mark that had almost right angle corners. Bruises usually have a tapering off—a softer edge where the color begins to fade." She brought a bent knuckle to her cheek under her once swollen eye. Even beneath the makeup, the outline of her injury was visible, and the marshals nodded in understanding.

The air nearly crackled with unspoken questions. Everyone wanted to ask if Julie could remember more, but she just kept shaking her head.

"I wish I had something else. Something that would really help."

"Oh, this has been a huge help." Serena pointed to the recorder. "We need to talk with Bud and Burke—"

"Bud and Burke?" The names meant nothing to Zach except that maybe their case was bigger than he'd guessed. He knew about the baby picked up in the Denver airport—probably the kid in the picture. And now Kay. Josh and Serena had mentioned multiple babies and other marshals on their last visit. At least two more men looking for missing children with who knew how many in the background. Just how big of a case had he stumbled upon?

"Bud Hollingsworth and Burke Trier." Josh pulled the recorder back to his side of the table before flipping it off. "They're with the marshals office and working with us on some cases that we think might be related."

The corner of Julie's eyes crinkled, her lips pursing. She pointed to the picture that Serena tucked into the front pocket of her folder. "To my case?" When they said nothing, she came to her own conclusion. "That baby is missing, too, isn't she?"

Apparently common sense and deductive reasoning weren't housed in the same area of the brain as long-term memory. Julie seemed to have no trouble unlocking those skills.

"Something like that." The marshals glanced at each other, their eyes locking for longer than necessary, and when Serena finally looked away, Josh's gaze hovered on her for a moment longer. It wasn't openly affectionate, nor was it emotionless. His eyes flickered with something like professional admiration.

The entire moment lasted less than a second before Josh turned back to his recorder. "We better get back on the road. But we'd like to hear if you remember anything else related to Kay or her mother."

"Of course." Julie eyed him like she wasn't quite sure if she wanted to trust him. Probably, like Zach, they couldn't talk about ongoing investigations, but that didn't mean Julie had to like it. She bestowed a genuine smile on Serena, and the room lit up, like the sky during a spring thunderstorm.

Zach jumped to his feet and gestured toward the door with a flat hand. "I'll walk you out." He didn't know when he'd become afraid of lightning, but he had to get out of there and get his head on straight before spending any more time with Julie and her smile.

The marshals gathered their things and moved toward the door. Zach turned the knob and pulled it open at the same moment that Serena spun back to Julie. "Would you look at one more picture for me?"

Julie's gaze sought him out—not exactly asking for permission, more for assurance. He gave her a quick nod, even though he had no idea what else Serena could be looking for. He had to trust this team or risk losing any help they might be able to offer. And risk missing out on finding Kay. That wasn't a gamble he could afford to take.

Serena pulled open her leather file one more time, flourishing the same five-by-seven that she had shown Julie less than a week before. "Are you sure you don't know this guy?"

Face turning red and eyes squinting hard, Julie focused on the face before her. "Frank Adams." She spoke the name in a hushed tone, running a finger over the placard at his chest. Her eyes seemed to caress his every line from the red slash across his chin to the angle of his dark hair. To Zach's left Josh held his breath while Serena leaned forward on her tiptoes.

"I'm sorry. I don't know him."

The sharp click of their heels as the marshals marched through the bull pen to the station's front door marked the rhythm of his new mantra. Find. Out. Who. Frank. Is.

They hadn't asked Julie to take a second look for her health. They'd wanted to see Julie's reaction to him because they thought Frank Adams was somehow involved. And if he was tied to their case, then there was a chance that he was tied to Julie's case.

It was past time to track the guy down.

Josh pushed open the glass door, ushering Serena through with a hand at the small of her back.

It wasn't just the sunlight that made him squint. Something was going on with these two.

"So how long have you been together?"

Serena's eyes popped open wider than they'd been. "Oh, we're not together," she said while Josh glanced at her out of the corner of his eye before scraping his toe across the asphalt drive in front of the station.

Jackpot. There was definitely something brewing between those two.

Holding in his chuckle, he covered himself. "I mean, how long have you been partners?"

Pink rushed up Serena's neck from under the collar of her white button-up, and she stared at the front of her folder like it held the codes to Fort Knox.

"Just a few months." Josh reached out to shake hands. "Good to see you again." His grip was firm. "Let us know if you hear anything."

"Will do."

Zach didn't wait for them to drive off before hurrying back inside, making a beeline for his desk. Picking up his phone, he punched in a familiar number. It rang three times before rolling over to voice mail.

"You got Phil. You know what to do."

After a long beep, Zach plastered a smile onto his face that he hoped made it into his voice. "It's Detective Jones. I need a little info on a guy you probably know. Call me back."

Julie counted every tree, studied every sidewalk crack and read every sign they passed. Green leaves had begun sprouting on the saplings along the street, their thin trunks bending beneath the weight of the wind. Dark lights lined the signs of the popular haunts, all of them foreign to her.

"Anything?"

It was only the third time in an hour of driving through downtown Minneapolis that Zach had asked. Even with a hopeful tone, the question grated on her. Maybe because she would do anything to be able to give the answer that he wanted to hear.

It was the answer she wanted to give, as well.

It just wasn't true.

Pressing her forehead against the cool pane of the passenger window, she squeezed her fists until her nails bit into her palms. "Not yet."

He sighed softly, like he didn't want her to hear his frustration. He'd been calm all morning, ever since asking her to go on a drive to see if they could jog her memory with a familiar location. Actually, the invitation had caught her off guard. He'd kept his distance for the past several days, checking in but never spending time alone with her.

Perfect. She'd scared him off with her almost kiss.

She wanted to knock her head against the window. Maybe that would help her memories return. Or at least knock out the recent embarrassing ones.

A knot in her stomach twisted; a voice in her head screamed that he just wanted her out of his house and his life.

"We'll find something that's familiar."

She chanced a look in his direction. His grin was genuine and a little lopsided, white teeth gleaming in the late morning sun.

He stopped at a light and pointed toward a row of night spots. "This is a pretty busy area after eight or so. Any of these facings ring a bell?"

They all had generic names like The Dive and Mom's Place. But the green door adorned with shamrocks and *McNulty's* emblazoned above it couldn't be ignored. It certainly drew her eye. She just couldn't be sure if it was because of the color or that Ramirez had mentioned it when she was at the station. Or that she'd been there.

"How far away is Webster Park?" His eyes flashed in her direction. "I'm not stupid. I know you have a hunch that I was right here that night."

He laughed, joining the flow of traffic again. "I never thought you were stupid. I just didn't think I was quite so transparent."

"Don't beat yourself up. It's not like you're a cop who needs a good poker face or anything."

His shoulders shook. "Glad to see that a knock on your head hasn't hurt your sarcasm even if you can't remember if you were sarcastic before."

She nearly smacked him in the arm. He was making fun of her amnesia. And she wanted to laugh. That wasn't fair.

Yet it was such a refreshing change.

"Thank you."

Snapping his head in her direction, he raised his eyebrows. "For what?"

"I guess there are too many things to list. But right now, thanks for not coddling me."

With a wink, he pulled onto the main road that took them out of the downtown district and past a big green sign announcing Webster Park. "Let's get out of here. Maybe we're in the wrong city altogether."

Zipping along in his sedan, the trees melded together, the buildings giving way to the peace of more rural Minnesota. Just for a minute. Her heart rate slowed, her chest rising and falling in an even, easy rhythm. When a fresh set of skyscrapers filled the horizon, a band tugged around her lungs. It didn't stop her from drawing a breath, but it wasn't quite as smooth as it had been.

"Welcome to Saint Paul." With a flourish of his hand, he indicated the entire city before them. "That's the Xcel Energy Center on your left, where the Wild play."

"The wild what?"

"The Minnesota Wild." Squinting at her, he shook his head. "Any self-respecting Minnesotan doesn't miss a hockey game."

"How do you know I'm from Minnesota?"

His jaw dropped, and he stared at her without blinking. She guessed that her expression mirrored his as they held eye contact for a long second. "What if you're not from here?" He spoke slowly and softly, the question and all of its follow-ups tumbling across his face. "I've been narrowing down missing-persons reports to Minnesota, but if you're not from here, that's why it's not showing up. I'll look again with a broader search as soon as I get back to the station."

This could change everything. There was no way to know for sure unless someone really was looking for her. But what if...

She let her mind wander to the possibilities as he turned onto a side street. A stunning hotel to their left boasted of the area's history and beauty. Its angled arms seemed to welcome guests with a hug. An iron portico covered a red carpet to the lobby doors, which were adorned with gilded scrollwork and handles. Doormen in top hats and white gloves greeted guests at their car doors.

The Saint Paul. Simple name for extravagant splendor.

Too bad she didn't remember ever staying there.

"I'd like to stay here someday."

"You and me both." He laughed. "But I'd have to make commissioner before I could afford that."

She shot him a glance as he turned again.

A historic, red-and-white railroad car sat on the sidewalk at the base of an office building. All the corners were curved, except the windows, which made up the top half of the wall all the way around. Several steps led up to a wall of rectangular windows, which framed an entrance at the center of the car. A lighted arrow at the top pointed to free parking, and the letters across the side of the car announced Mickey's Diner.

Her stomach clenched, fire erupting through her temple. Images flashed across her mind's eye, gritty and not fully formed. She grabbed for Zach's arm, needing something stable.

He shot a look at her hands, then into her face. "What's wrong?"

Tongue stuck to the roof of her mouth, she could only point at the diner with a frantic finger.

He turned in the direction she indicated. "Mickey's? Are you hungry? I could eat some lunch."

"No." Squeezing her eyes closed and forcing her mouth to form the words, she said, "I *know* that place."

TEN

Zach slammed on the brakes, jerking against his seat belt and getting a long honk from the car behind him for it. Ignoring the other driver, he whipped an inadvisable U-turn around a low median and tore into the parking lot next to the famous diner. It had just emptied out following the lunch rush, and he pulled into an open space near the end of the diner car.

With the car safely in Park, he took a shaky breath before turning toward Julie. "What did you just say?"

Her eyes were bigger than usual, unblinking. She was seeing something beyond what was right in front of them. She'd had the same look when she'd seen the mom and baby at church the previous Sunday.

What was she seeing? He desperately wanted to ask, but he couldn't risk interrupting the thoughts and memories as they formed, so he drummed his fingers on the steering wheel while his knee bounced. Shooting up a prayer that this would break open the case and remind her who she was, he waited.

After an eternity of silence, save for the late lunch-takers motoring in and out around them, she blinked. Her lips pursed as though to speak, but then relaxed. Again she began and stopped herself. And finally in a hushed tone,

"I don't know if I've ever been here before, but I know I know this place." Her shoulders rose as she glanced in his direction. "I think I might have been here with a man."

His stomach dropped. "Was it Frank Adams?" *Or her husband?* He couldn't give voice to the second question, and he sure didn't want to analyze why.

"I don't think so. He had dark hair, but he wasn't..." She cocked her head to the side, eyes again trained on the red stripes around the diner's curved white edges. "I think he might have been my..."

Her pause made his heart pound three times as hard as normal. Deep breathing did nothing to release the tension building in his chest, so he plastered a fake smile in place, hoping she wouldn't notice how hard he had to work to keep it there.

"I think it was my dad."

It was more question than statement, but it did the trick. Blood rushed through him, setting his fingers tingling and letting his lungs expand.

"Can you tell me his name?"

"No." She shot him a sideways glance and a sheepish shrug. "This remembering in bits and pieces isn't doing us much good, is it?"

"Hey, you're doing great. Every memory is one closer to remembering what happened to Kay and who attacked you." That earned him a grin that made his stomach warm. "Want to go inside and see if it brings up any other memories?"

"Yes."

They walked the several steps up to the red front door, and as he opened it for her, he pressed a hand to the small of her back. She led the way into the single room. To the right sat a few red-and-white booths. To the left there was a long shining counter with fifteen-or-so red vinyl stools.

Steel shelves and warming pans and stoves lined the wall on the far side of the counter.

A cook in all-white, his apron stained with the day's special, looked up from where he slung hash browns. "Welcome to Mickey's. Grab a seat at the counter."

Julie didn't have to be told twice, heading straight for the only two adjacent empty stools. Plopping down on one, she smiled at a waitress in a classic, pink diner uniform. Her white collar and cuffs on her sleeves were pristine. Her once all-white apron had a brown streak across the front, but at least her uniform was in better shape than her counterpart's.

"I'm Marge," she said, plopping a menu in front of each of them. Leaning her elbows on the counter, she rested her chin on her hands. "Ever been to Mickey's before?"

Zach glanced at Julie before she said, "I think so."

"Well, then, welcome back." She winked a faded blue eye below long blond bangs. "Take a look at the menu, and I'll be right back."

Marge bustled away, taking a plate from the cook and sliding it in front of the guy sitting next to Julie. He dug into an enormous hamburger with two patties and oozing with melted cheese.

Zach wanted that.

Julie took a little longer to decide, her gaze shooting around the interior of the car, analyzing the wooden panels and red vinyl. Occasionally her eyes drifted toward the windows and the buzzing street just beyond.

"All right, you two, what's it going to be?" Marge said, still halfway down the row, picking up plates and an empty ketchup bottle on her way toward them.

Julie's eyebrows pinched together. "Pancakes. Lots of them."

Marge chuckled. "You want eggs or bacon with those?"

"Nope. Just pancakes."

"And I want whatever that guy's having." Zach pointed to their neighbor, who nodded in agreement.

Julie leaned toward the man's elbow, squinting at the melting mess of goodness. "What is that?"

"Mickey's Sputnick," Marge supplied. "It's a classic, and just about as life-changing as space travel."

"I'll testify to that," their neighbor said around a big bite of burger.

"Is that a favorite of yours?" Julie asked.

"Sure is. I come in here at least once a week for one of these."

Julie made a minimal sound of curiosity.

"Absolutely. Best burger in the area."

"And you work around here?"

"Yep." He pointed out the window. "I manage the box office at the Xcel Center."

A genuine smile lit Julie's features. "The Wild."

"That's right. You ever come to the games?"

"Umm...not really."

The guy bit off another hunk of meat, shoving it into the corner of his mouth before continuing, "It's a good job. I like it." He swallowed after two chews, and Zach half expected to have to do the Heimlich to save the guy's life. "I mean, it's not what I want to do forever, but it pays the bills. And the hours aren't too bad. Plus, I get to see the hockey games. And I can walk down here for a Sputnick whenever I need it."

Marge slipped their plates in place, and Julie poured syrup over her pancakes in a perfect spiral while asking, "So what is a forever kind of job?"

"I'd really like to run a bait-and-tackle shop."

Zach couldn't see her face, as Julie had her back to him, but she must have looked confused, as the other guy explained.

"Fishing gear and stuff. My buddy Gary and me want to open a store with stuff for year-round fishing. Maybe even sell shanties for ice fishing. We've been fishing together since we were kids. Lived next door to each other and my dad took us out to the lake every weekend. But I don't get out there as much as we used to."

Julie's new friend rambled on about the types of fish he liked to catch, which ones were best for eating and what he and Gary were going to call their shop.

She nodded at the details, cutting into her stack of pancakes without even looking at them. The smell of maple and butter surrounded them as she took her first bite.

Zach should take her with him when he had to talk with witnesses and suspects. She hadn't done a thing but show a little interest, and the guy was pouring out his entire life story. Zach's investigations never went quite that smoothly.

Marge wandered by, raising an eyebrow at him.

Sliding open his jacket to reveal his badge without announcing it to anyone else, he quirked an eyebrow. She looked up and down the row of stool-dwellers before stepping toward him.

"Can I help you with something?" Her voice was low enough that he had to catch more than half her words by reading her very pink lips.

He ticked his head toward Julie. "You ever seen her here before?"

"Her?" Marge's forehead shifted with deep, uneven wrinkles. "I don't think so."

"How about your cook? He seen her?"

She stepped away, whispered to the man in the white paper hat and pointed in Zach's general direction. The cook looked up from the flipper in his hand and gave Julie a long look. The corners of his mouth angled down, and he shook his head.

So Julie remembered Mickey's, but the staff, who had clearly been here for at least a century, didn't know her. What was her connection to this place?

The phone in his pocket vibrated. Pulling it out, he checked to see who was calling. The screen said only *Unlisted.* Tapping Julie's shoulder, he interrupted her conversation with the fisherman.

"I'll be right back."

"Okay." She glanced at his phone and back up at him. "Everything all right?"

"Yeah, I'm just going to take this outside." He slipped out the door and past a couple headed up the stairs. Around the corner of the diner, he could still see Julie through the window as he answered the call. "This is Jones."

"Hey. It's Phil." The man sniffed loudly. "I got your message. What's up?"

"Took you long enough to call me back."

"Hey, man. You want me to call you back or not? Some of us have lives and stuff."

Right. A life. That's what he called spending every day looking for his next hit, crashing on a dealer's couch or at a shelter, if he was lucky. That wasn't a real life. Real life was doing something that mattered. Something that made someone else's life better.

He caught Julie's profile out of the corner of his eye as she threw her head back, laughing at something her new friend had said. Oh, man, she was beautiful. All flashing brown eyes and full cherry lips. And the way she leaned in to really listen to the man who meant nothing more to her than a fellow diner.

Oh, she was trusting. She'd believed him when he promised that he'd help her, promised to keep her safe.

Now he just had to make good on that vow.

And that meant getting whatever he could out of his informant. "Whatever you say, Phil. I just need to know how to get in touch with someone you probably know."

"What's it to ya?" His syllables were soft, slurred together from too much to drink, no doubt. Once a world-class thief, drugs and alcohol had turned Phil into a shell of the man he'd been. He jumped at his own shadow now. But he still knew who was who in illegal dealings in the Twin Cities.

"What do you need?"

Phil's laugh was hoarse and filled with phlegm. "What I need, you refuse to give me."

"That's because it's still against the law."

"Sure." Zach could almost hear the shrug in the other man's voice. "You got a sleeping bag or something? It's still pretty cold at night down by the river."

"Maybe. You ever heard of a guy named Frank Adams?"

"Frank?"

A gust of wind kicked up his jacket, and he slipped his chain holding his badge inside his shirt. "Yeah. I heard he's from these parts, and he might be working a job. You know where I can find him?"

"Nah. Keep your sleeping bag. I don't even need blow that bad."

Well, that escalated quickly. "What?"

"I can't help you. Call me next time you're looking for someone who won't tear what's left of my teeth out if I rolled on him."

The line went dead, and he stared at the screen on his phone for a long time. What on earth just happened? Apparently Frank Adams was more notorious than he'd suspected. How had he never heard of the guy? He clearly had a street rep and probably a rap sheet to match.

Maybe Phil would talk to him in person. The promise of a warm place to stay for the night—even if it was a jail cell—might entice the guy. But tracking Phil down wasn't always as easy as just wishing to find the guy.

Pressing a single button to call the station, he checked on Julie again. She'd drawn Marge into the conversation with Fish Man.

"MPD, this is Hazel."

"Hey, it's Jones."

"Well, well, Detective. You never call. You never write."

"I've been too afraid you wouldn't write back." Flirting with a woman at least twice his age. What was his world coming to? He'd rather it was Julie.

The realization knocked the wind out of him, and he had to lean against the side of the railcar to keep his feet. He had to solve this case. Fast.

And then what?

And then Julie would go back to wherever she should be. Wherever she didn't make him wish so hard that they'd met under different circumstances.

Working Homicide was hard on a man. It was harder on the woman he cared about. Julie deserved better than half his attention, better than haunted nights and pain-filled days. He had to send her back to her home.

"What can I do for you?" Hazel asked.

"Can you trace the call that just came through my cell phone?"

Her fingers punched the keyboard on her end of the call with a ferocity that suggested the keyboard had insulted her. "This'll take just a minute."

"I'll wait."

Julie provided a pleasant distraction for an instant before he reminded himself that he had to stop thinking about her as anything other than a witness in his protection. She wasn't staying, and as long as he was thinking about what it would be like if she was, he risked missing a clue or a lead that could wrap her case and put the man responsible behind bars.

"It looks like it originated at a pay phone."

"Seriously? Are those still around?"

"A few of them." She gave him the address and the number for the phone, and he scribbled it into his notepad.

"Thanks, Hazel."

"Call me anytime, young man."

Pocketing his phone as he stepped back inside, he plopped onto his seat and popped a cold French fry into his mouth.

Julie spun toward him and raised her eyebrows to ask her question without saying a word.

"I need to run an errand."

"All right. Let's go."

He tossed enough money on the counter to cover their lunch bill and a generous tip for Marge. "Thanks, hon!" she called as they left the same way they'd come in.

On the road back to his place, he said, "I'm going to drop you off at home, all right?"

"Okay." Her lips pursed to the side, and she didn't sound as positive as her response suggested.

"I need to go see someone about the case."

She sat up a little straighter. "Can I go with you?"

"No."

The silence was thicker than a redwood, apparently neither of them eager to cut it. He didn't want to go into detail with her, and he certainly couldn't invite her to meet with a junkie informant about a man who may or may not have tried to kill her at least three times.

As he pulled into his conspicuously empty driveway, he pulled on the door handle.

"Listen, Samantha should be home soon. I'm sorry I can't take you with me."

She twisted toward him, long lashes fluttering over her doe eyes. "I thought we were in thi-is together." The catch in her voice lit a flame of fear in her eyes that tugged at his chest.

"You'll be fine here. Just lock the door, don't answer it if anyone knocks and keep your phone with you. Gizmo is probably downstairs sleeping. Wake him up if you need some company."

When her eyes dropped toward the center console, he couldn't stop his hand from reaching out to cup her cheek and tuck her hair behind her ear. Maybe it was his imagination, but she seemed to lean into his embrace for just a moment before pulling back, swinging her legs out of the car.

"I'll be right back. And I'll call a black-and-white to drive down the street a few times until Samantha gets back."

She nodded and rushed to the front door, unlocking it and slipping inside without a glance over her shoulder.

He slammed the car into Reverse as he called the station to request a drive-by, backing into the street before the clench in his gut convinced him not to leave her alone. She'd be fine. His sister would be home in a few minutes, and no one knew she was staying with them anyway.

She'd be just fine.

So why was he working so hard to persuade himself?

Julie pressed her back flat against the front door, checking again to make sure that the key had twisted far enough to engage the lock. Jiggling the handle, she checked one last time. Stuck.

Just like Zach had said. She was fine.

Maybe she should check the back door, just to be safe.

The late winter sun had warmed the house through the big bay window in the living room, but as it set, shadows danced across the room. She skipped and hopped with each shape-shifting illusion, reaching a dead run halfway down the hall. Her heart beating a cadence that threatened to send it flying out of her chest, she slammed into the back door, pressing hands flat against two of the nine small windows that made up the top half of the door.

She peered hard into the growing darkness of the backyard but could make out only the pile of wood against the side fence. Something moved beside it, and she jerked on the key stuck in the interior lock. It didn't budge. She tried the knob. It rattled, but held.

No one was going to get inside tonight unless they had a key.

Besides, no one was going to try to get in. No one knew she was staying with Zach's family.

"Quit being so silly."

Her self-reprimand didn't slow the rush of blood that made her skin feel too tight and her temples throb.

Finding Gizmo would help. Tiptoeing down the stairs toward Zach's domain, she listened for the dog, his great snores bouncing up the walls. Well, he wasn't going to be good company. Closing the door against the coolness of the basement behind her, she spun in a slow circle in the middle of the kitchen.

Maybe a hot cup of tea would help. As she filled the teapot with water, a dog barked next door, and she dropped the pot. The noise was enough to wake even Keaton, who often snored heavily on the couch after a night shift.

If only he were snoring there now.

But he wasn't. The house was oddly silent without the Jones siblings teasing and hollering at each other.

Despite a shaking hand, she managed to light one of the gas burners and set the teapot into place. Crossing her arms, she stared at it. Nothing happened. Probably nothing would happen as long as she hovered over it.

Pulling a mug from the cupboard and setting a tea bag into it, she carried it to the far window overlooking the breakfast nook. The last of the big oak tree's shadows had disappeared, and she reached for the light switch. The room awash in light, she couldn't see anything but her own reflection in the window, so she flipped it off again.

Nothing but rustling grass out there.

She slammed the curtains closed anyway and turned the overhead back on.

The teapot whistled. Jumping, she nearly dropped her mug, juggling it twice before catching it.

Great. Now she was scared of a little noise. What next? Puppies and kittens?

Just because this was her first time all alone since the car crash—since the hospital actually—didn't give her liberty to lose her mind. Or assume that another attack was right around the corner. But it wouldn't hurt to have a little backup.

She glanced at her phone, wishing it would ring. Maybe she could just give Zach a call. But she tamped down that urge as soon as it welled within her. He was doing important work. Work that might find Kay. Work that might solve her own case.

Now was not the time to let her imagination get the better of her.

"Just let him do his job," she chided herself, before scooping up her phone and wandering toward the living room.

Settling into Keaton's favorite couch spot, she turned on the television and blew into the steaming mug. Both hands were wrapped around the warm ceramic more to keep them from shaking than from the cold. Tucking her legs beneath her, she sank into the corner of the sofa, the back and an arm holding her up.

Lucy and Ethel were in the middle of another black-and-white catastrophe when the front door handle jiggled.

Julie nearly missed it for the laughter from the audience on the show. But it squeaked a little and then stopped.

Her heart leaped to her throat, and she set her mug down. "Samantha?" More croak than not, she cleared her throat and tried again. "Samantha, is that you?"

No response.

Maybe it was the wind rattling the old house.

The knot in her stomach quickly squashed that dream.

Holding the curtains back, she peeked out the window next to the front door just in time to see a dark shadow disappear around the corner of the building, headed for the backyard.

Scrambling for her phone, she dialed Samantha's number, which went immediately to voice mail. She must be on her way. She had to be.

Julie set her phone on the end table and picked up her tea again, her gaze never wavering from the black screen as she battled the urge to call Zach. But that would interrupt him while he was working the case. Her case.

Glancing toward the ceiling, she prayed for deliverance, but fear seemed to strangle even the thinnest threads of hope. "God, I need You." The words died on the tip of her tongue. God still felt like a distant figure, like someone she hadn't spoken with in far too long. How had she let Him get so far away? He'd been so close just a few days before in church. Where was He now when she needed Him?

Something clattered in the back of the house.

She couldn't wait for Samantha. There was someone out there. Punching the emergency call button on the landline phone, she wrapped her arms around her knees as she waited for the operator to pick up.

"Nine-one-one. What's your emergency?"

The words caught on her constricted throat, and she had to push them through the fear. "Someone's trying to break into the house."

"What's your address?"

Blurting out the location of Zach's home, she tried to calm the tremors that threatened to dump her tea in her lap.

"An officer is on his way. Please stay on—"

The line went dead, as cold as the chills racing down her arms.

A crash on the back porch set Gizmo to barking in the basement and had her out of her seat and scrambling for something—anything—she might be able to use to defend herself. Out of the corner of her eye, she caught sight of Reese's hockey stick leaning into the corner by the stairs, waiting to be taken to his room. If someone was on the back porch, maybe the hockey stick would scare him off.

Snatching it to her chest, she flew toward the back door to make sure it hadn't been breached, skidding to a halt before the window panels.

She jerked toward the curtains covering the window. If her attacker was back for another round, she had to know where he was. Knowing was better than not.

And then a pane on the back door shattered, and she fell to the ground.

ELEVEN

Julie covered her head with her hands and screamed as glass showered over her. The shards peppered her back, and when they stopped, she risked a glance toward the door, where a black-gloved hand slithered through the hollow of the broken window.

Heart pounding and ears ringing, she pushed herself up, rushing toward the fingers that grazed the interior key still in the lock. If he unlocked the door, she'd be dead. She didn't doubt that.

She didn't really have any choice but to fight back. There was no time to go for her phone or wait for help.

God, save me!

She swung the hockey stick toward the door, chanting the phrase over and over in her mind. Slashing awkwardly at the disembodied arm, she battled for control of the key. If she could just swipe his hand out of the way, she could get the key out of the lock.

The tips of her fingers had just pinched the edge of the key when the black glove grabbed her weapon, wrenching it enough to throw her off balance, sending her head slamming against the immobile frame.

White lights flashed before her eyes as fire blazed a trail across her scalp.

"Let me in!"

His growl was enough to keep her fighting. Yanking her arm, she nearly dislodged his grip on her elbow. He shifted his stance, and she saw his face for the first time— or rather the ski mask that covered it. But the sneer in the mouth opening couldn't be denied.

Baring her nails, she dug into his arm, which was protected by a leather jacket.

Like the one the guy on the motorcycle had been wearing.

"Let go of me." Her words were hoarse; her throat burned. Had she been screaming? The entire night ran together in one mad scramble as another window smashed, his other arm snaking through the opening to grab her hair.

Her head snapped back, tears flooding her eyes as the pain registered off the charts.

Gizmo's sharp cries and scratches at the basement entrance only added to the cacophony.

"Let. Go!" She coughed and sputtered as he pulled her against the wall, banging her head again.

As quickly as he'd grabbed her, he let go.

Julie crumpled to the ground, her attacker's clomping footfalls ringing down the back porch and vanishing as the front door swung open.

A gust of cold wind swept down the hall, leaving goose bumps up and down her arms. Or maybe it was the relief that she wasn't alone anymore and that the masked man had taken off.

"Julie?"

From her kneeling position amid the broken glass, she looked toward the voice.

Samantha, arms full of grocery bags, stared at her as though she couldn't understand what she was seeing. Then she dropped everything and rushed forward. "Julie!"

"Careful." Julie's shoulders couldn't hold her up any

longer, and she slumped forward, bending at the waist. "Broken glass."

"What happened?" Samantha's question came out on a breath, her eyes wide and mouth agape.

Julie pointed toward the door with one hand; the other rested on the floor by her knee. "He tried to break in. Tried to unlock the door." She swallowed, her throat raw. "Grabbed me."

"Okay." A professional calm passed over her face as Samantha straightened her shoulders. "Do you need an ambulance? I can have one here in four minutes."

"No." She didn't want to go back to the hospital. "Nothing's broken. I'm not bleeding. Already called nine-one-one."

Samantha squatted in front of her, running a thumb over Julie's forehead. Pain flared, and she jerked away. "It looks like you bumped your head pretty good. Are you dizzy?" Just inches away, Samantha had to raise her voice over Gizmo's frantic cries.

"Just—" She tried to lift an arm, but it flopped back to her side. "Just tired."

"Come on." Samantha slipped an arm around Julie's back, helping her stand and shuffle three feet to the bench next to the table in the breakfast nook. "Your adrenaline is fading, and you might be going into shock."

"It's not shock." Julie sank onto the bench, resting elbows on the table and her head in her hands.

Samantha spoke into her cell phone, but Julie couldn't make out any distinct words, just the low hum of talking and barking at the door leading to the basement, all below the high-pitched buzzing that echoed in her ears.

"Whoa. Slow down." Zach did the opposite of his directive to his sister, slamming his gas pedal to the floor. His car lurched in response.

"Someone tried to break in and get his hands on Julie."

Like a stone in the lake, his heart sank. "Is she hurt?" Still three miles from home, he zipped between traffic, swerving around slower cars and staring hard at the road. If he didn't, he was liable to slam into another vehicle, a risk he couldn't take.

He had to get back to Julie.

"I don't think so," Samantha said. "Pretty shaky, but in one piece. She did get hit in the head."

"Call an ambulance." She needed to be checked out again. There was no telling what kind of damage a bump on the head could cause.

Samantha skirted the subject. "Uniforms are already on their way to take an official statement, and they'll bring the crime scene guys to check for prints."

A murmur in the background sounded, and Samantha was silent for a long moment.

"What? What's going on?"

"Julie said that he had on black gloves. She's sure there won't be any prints."

Zach slammed on his brakes at a red light, glaring at it until it flipped to green and he could sail through the intersection. "How did he get inside?" His throat constricted on the last word, leaving it mostly unspoken.

Why hadn't he taken Julie with him? He hadn't found Phil anyway. The phone booth and surrounding area had been deserted.

And if she'd been with him, she wouldn't have been at home.

Alone.

Attacked.

God, forgive me. I promised I'd keep her safe, and I've failed in every possible way.

"Well, he didn't get all the way in." Samantha sounded

as surprised as he was at her words. "He broke out a couple little windows on the back door and tried to unlock it, but Julie fought him off with a hockey stick."

"Oh, Lord," he breathed the prayer, a cry for mercy and guidance and Julie's safety all rolled into two words.

"It looks like he got a hold of her arm and pulled her against the door, which is when she hit her head. But she's alert and physically in pretty good shape."

"I'm almost home. I'll be there in three minutes." Two if he floored it through the next light.

A hubbub on the other end of the line sent his blood pressure rising.

"Samantha, what's going on?"

"Oh, Keaton just got home. I'll see you in a sec." She hung up without any other warning, and he could do nothing but pray the last four blocks home.

It seemed like an eternity before he pulled into the driveway beside Keaton's old truck. He was out of the car before it was all the way in Park, running for the front door, down the hall and to Julie's side.

Falling to his knees before her, he placed one hand on her knee, needing to know that she wasn't going to disappear before his eyes. With his other hand he cupped her cheek. "I'll take you to the hospital right now if you need."

She blinked tired eyes, touching the back of his hand with tentative fingers. "I don't want to go back there."

He didn't blame her. He wouldn't want to go, either. Especially knowing that she'd been attacked there once already.

His lips flattened into a hard line, but he nodded. "How's your head? Samantha said you got another knock on it."

She managed to brush her short bangs out of the way, revealing an already purple bruise. Then she lifted one corner of her mouth. "Well, another bump on the head didn't shake my memories loose like I was hoping it would."

His chuckle caught him by surprise, almost as much as hers did.

"You think you're pretty funny, huh?"

She nodded, her lips quivering with humor and fading adrenaline. "Kind of."

He couldn't tear his gaze away from her mouth, pink and perfect. He'd never wanted to kiss a woman as much as he did in that moment.

For a second it didn't matter that she didn't know her past. For a second it didn't faze him that she wasn't going to be around after her memory returned and that he had no business being attracted to her.

For one brief second it didn't even register that she wasn't his.

His fingers curled into her hair, and he leaned in. Her eyes grew wide, her mouth falling open just a breath.

So much grace in one woman. Whatever she'd been like before the attack in Webster Park, he didn't care. In this moment she was exactly the kind of woman he'd been waiting to meet.

A moment away from sealing the kiss, his brother clapped him on the shoulder. "The uniforms are ready to talk with Julie."

Zach jerked back, nearly falling onto his backside. He'd completely ignored the presence of not only his brother but also his sister, who stood on the opposite side of the room. Her arms crossed, she shot him a knowing smirk.

That could have gone better.

That was also the understatement of the century.

In a perfect world, he'd have been able to kiss Julie soundly without interruption from his family. He'd have been able to hold her close as his heart thundered in his chest.

And he wouldn't have to keep himself from jumping into a real relationship with her just because he had to give her back to wherever she belonged.

Wherever that was.

And whenever that moment came, it would be too soon.

A very young woman in a blue uniform entered the kitchen, keeping her distance and eyeing them both with a curious glance. Zach didn't know her, so she'd probably joined the department after he'd transferred to Homicide.

Giving Julie's knee one more squeeze, he rose to his feet and introduced himself. "Detective Jones. Homicide."

Her eyes grew large, and she shook his hand. "Georgia Singletary. We were called in about an attempted home invasion."

He pointed her to Julie, introduced them and then stepped back, never letting her out of his sight. Taking several deep breaths, he tried to even his restless heartbeat and calm the screaming in his mind. He should have been with her.

He wouldn't make that mistake again.

By the time Officer Singletary had completed the interview, the crime scene team had checked for evidence and the house had cleared out, Julie was ready to crawl into bed and forget that the world existed. Just for eight blissful hours, maybe no one would hunt her, she wouldn't hold locked memories of a missing child and Zach would have kissed her.

But wishing didn't make it so. Especially not that last wish.

She was still just a stray, still just someone he had helped because of his kind spirit.

That hadn't been an almost kiss.

A tiny voice in the back of her mind told her that wasn't quite true.

All right, maybe it *was* almost a kiss. But it was most likely pity-induced. Any real feelings growing between them were entirely one-sided. *Her*-sided.

There was no sense in wishing her reality away. All she really had was the man standing before her. And maybe a memory that would help locate baby Kay. If she could just find that memory.

Zach held up the half-empty tea kettle that had still been on the burner. "How about a cup of tea while I clean up this glass?"

She'd left her mug…somewhere. But where? She spun in a slow circle, trying to retrace her steps before the broken window, but the entire night was about as clear as a Midwest blizzard.

"What do you need?" he asked, guiding her back to her seat.

"I'm okay." Just as the words escaped, her toe caught on the back of her heel. She stumbled into him. His arms wrapped around her back, nearly lifting her onto the bench by the table. And completely stealing her breath.

What was it about this guy? Why did he make her feel like she'd never met an attractive man before?

She needed to put some space between them.

Scooting back, she wrapped her arms around her stomach. "I'm good. Just looking for my mug."

"I'll get it for you." He strolled around the pile of glass in the middle of the floor, filled up the kettle and set it to warming on the burner's low flame.

When he walked out of the room and down the hall, the temperature seemed to drop. Maybe it was the wind blowing through the broken windows. More likely it was the flashes of a black glove reaching through those frames that her mind had no trouble conjuring.

With every blink the image reappeared.

And with it the coiling tightness in her stomach and the band around her lungs.

Her arm twitched, and those brutish fingers were around her elbow again. He smelled of fresh leather and something woodsy—outdoorsy—and his sneer had curdled her blood. His teeth were yellow, the front one chipped at the corner.

"Zach."

"Be right there." A door squeaked, and he appeared with a broom and dustpan in hand. "What is it?"

"He had a chipped tooth."

He looked toward the door, his frown growing pronounced. "What about the guy at the hospital? Did he have a chipped tooth, too?"

Biting into her lip, she stared at the ceiling until the images from that night formed. "I don't know. I never really saw his mouth. I do know he had blond hair, but he came at me at such an awkward angle that I didn't get a good look at his face."

He squatted down to sweep the larger shards of glass into the dustpan. His gaze turned serious, very focused on his work. "Frank Adams didn't have blond hair or a chipped tooth." Zach brushed some glass into the pan.

"He wasn't smiling in his mug shot, so I haven't seen his teeth." Julie paused for a long moment sorting every piece of evidence into place in her mind. "I suppose it could have been him tonight, but I don't think it was."

"If it's not Frank, who's after you?" His mumbled words as he reached for a large piece of glass were clearly not meant for her, but they sure posed an interesting question.

"Could he be working with someone else?"

"Ow!" Zach jerked his hand to his chest, cradling it in the other.

"Did you cut yourself?"

He held out his hand, a jagged red stripe growing between his thumb and forefinger.

She fell to the floor in front of him, pressing her fingers against the wound and calling for Keaton. When he appeared, she asked, "Do you have a first-aid kit?"

"Sure." He disappeared down the hall, and she called after him.

"Can you bring me a clean towel, too?"

Eye to eye with Zach and unable to tear her gaze away, she swallowed the urge to babble.

"I'll be fine. Really," he said.

"I know you will, but let me take a look at it anyway."

Something not far from humor glinted in Zach's eye as Keaton returned with a towel and the box, which bore a large red cross. She took the towel and wrapped it firmly around Zach's hand. Then she dug gauze and antibiotic ointment from the kit.

With quick and proficient movements, she cleaned the cut, washing away drying blood and revealing a long but shallow wound. "Oh, this looks good. It's not going to need stitches."

As she slathered ointment on it, the weight of Zach's gaze on top of her bent head seemed to increase. It sent a shiver crawling down her spine, and she fought the urge to look up until she'd finished wrapping his wound.

Finally done, she narrowed her eyes and glanced into his face. "What?"

"How did you know that?"

"Know what?"

He lifted his shoulder. "That I don't need stitches. How to clean it and wrap it like that."

Her eyes shot toward Keaton, hoping he'd have the answer to his brother's question, but he was too busy watching their exchange with barely concealed amusement.

Meeting Zach's gaze again, she shook her head. "I have no idea."

A chuckle burst out, and he covered his mouth with his uninjured hand as though he didn't know where it had come from and wanted to stop another from escaping. It didn't help. His laughter grew despite his fingers pressed to his lips, shoulders shaking and eyes watering.

And she didn't really have a choice. It was contagious, so she joined him.

Giggles swept over her like a spring rain, cool and cleansing.

Soon she couldn't catch her breath, the guffaws rolling in wave after wave. Zach's deeper chuckles added a harmony and rhythm to her higher-pitched melody.

Sinking to the floor, they leaned against each other until the tension of the evening, the stress of the day, the strain of the week fell away.

They were shoulder to shoulder and panting by the time she realized that Keaton had left them to their insanity, the door to the top-floor apartment squeaking loud enough to fill the entire house.

"I think I needed that," he said.

She smiled up at him, resting an ear against his shoulder. "Me, too." The effort required to hold her head upright squirmed just beyond her grasp, so she stayed snuggled into his side. Laughing with him was almost as nice as being held in his arms.

Almost.

After a long moment where the only noise was Samantha's hair dryer somewhere else in the house, she risked asking the question that kept bouncing through her mind. "What are we going to do?"

His shoulder stiffened, but he didn't pull away. "I'm going to patch up the broken windows."

"And after that?"

He let out a slow sigh. "We're going to find your memories. There's a mom out there somewhere who's missing her child, and you're the only one with any answers. And until we find them and the man coming after you, we have to keep you safe."

"How?"

He shook his head slowly, his gaze wandering down the hall. "We start with making sure you're never alone, and that we have a uniform watching the house at all times."

She just had to stay safe until her memories came back. If she couldn't get the memories out, then she was useless. And she wasn't about to be a worthless part of the search. She just had to find a familiar place that jogged her memory even more than Mickey's had.

"Is there some place here that everyone knows, that everyone's been to?"

He squinted at her, his eyes nearly disappearing. "What makes you ask that?"

"Just wondering what other places I should visit to see if I recognize them."

He glanced at the ceiling and leaned his head back. "I guess everyone's been to the Mall of America."

She nodded, chewing on a fingernail.

"Do you want to go there tomorrow?"

"I'm supposed to see the doctor again tomorrow afternoon to check up on my wrist and my head." She lifted her right hand, which had been in a brace until her last day in the hospital. "Maybe in the morning before I see the doctor?"

"All right. I'll take you then. On one condition."

Her stomach churned in a mix of curiosity and dread. "What's that?"

"You have to stay by my side…"

The rest of his sentence, though unspoken, was louder than any of his other words.

Because a man who would risk attacking her at the home of four cops wouldn't let up until he got what he wanted.

TWELVE

Zach rapped twice on the door to Julie's bedroom the next morning as Samantha walked by, headed for the second-floor bathroom. She quirked her eyebrow at him, her eyes teasing.

"It's a bit early to be bothering her, don't you think?"

He waved his phone in his hand. "Got to go into the station for something, so we're going to have to change our plans."

"Sure."

His sister still treated him like he was a college kid just trying to meet a nice girl. Well, he had met a nice girl. Finally.

She just had to go back to her own family soon.

When Julie opened the door, the hair on the right side of her head stood straight on end. She brushed a hand over it, flattening it only for a second before it sprang back to its most vibrant life. Eyes droopy with sleep and cheeks pink, she fumbled to tie the belt around an old robe on loan from Samantha. It was about three sizes too big and pooled at her wrists, nearly hiding her hands.

She smacked her mouth a few times, running her tongue across her teeth, and squinted up at him. "Mornin'."

Wow, she was cute in the morning.

He shook the thought away. It wasn't safe territory. Getting too attached could hurt. Every rescued puppy and wounded kitten he'd taken in had taken a tiny piece of his heart with them when he'd had to let them go.

The only difference with Julie was that she had the potential to take his whole heart.

"Good morning." He smiled. "How are you feeling today?"

Lifting her arm until her sleeve drooped to her elbow, she showed off a solid bruise just below the joint. "A few bumps and scrapes, but I don't think the doctor will be concerned about these."

"He'll probably just be concerned that you can't seem to stay out of trouble long enough to really get better."

She closed one eye, the other following the lines of his face. "And whose fault—" She bit down hard, stopping her words.

But he knew exactly what she had been thinking, and it ate at him. Of course it was his fault that she'd been alone last night. He hadn't expected Samantha to take a shopping trip or his fruitless search for Phil to last so long. Or that Phil would show up in the drunk tank that morning with a broken hand and no desire to talk about the details of what had happened.

A pang shot through his belly, and he pushed it down. He couldn't do a thing about what happened to Julie the night before except go out and find the guy responsible.

"Listen, I got a call from the station. I need to go in to take care of something."

From sleepy to brilliant, her eyes changed in a flash. "Do they have a lead? Do they know where Kay—" Again she cut herself off, her brows furrowing as she pulled away.

"What's going on?"

"I had a dream. I think it was about Lonnie and Kay."

"What happened in it?" He rested a hand around her shoulder, urging her back toward him. "What happened to Lonnie?"

"She was scared. She was so scared." Julie covered his hand with hers. "You have to find them. I know they're in trouble."

"I'm going to try right now. But I need you to stay here. Reese and Samantha will be here all day with you. I just need you to stay put until I come back for you. Then we'll go to the mall."

"All right."

Wrapping an arm around her shoulders, he pulled her in for a quick hug, and her hands snaked around his waist, clinging to his shirt.

He let her go before he could do something he'd regret and hustled down the stairs without looking back. One glance and he might change his mind and go back for her. But she couldn't come with him.

Out the door and on the road, he flipped his phone to the hands-free set and called an old friend. The phone rang five times before someone picked up. "Oasis."

"LeRoy Tibbets."

It was all the greeting that his high school friend needed. "Zach Jones. How are you? Heard you finally made detective and joined Homicide. Is that why you never come around to see me anymore?"

Zach laughed. He'd made detective more than three years before, but every time he saw LeRoy, he got the same ribbing. "How's the Oasis?"

"Broke but busy. Had seventy-three guys here last night."

While doing a stint in prison for his own drug problem, LeRoy had found God, given up the bad habits and promised to make a difference when he was released. LeRoy's first month on the outside, Zach had helped him start a little shelter for guys looking to get clean and sober. In just five years, three cots in a one-bedroom apartment had turned into a full-scale rehab program and homeless shelter.

LeRoy hadn't ever gone back to the addiction that put him behind bars, but he still had connections with those who hadn't been as strong. He was pretty much guaranteed to know someone who knew just about anyone that Zach could be looking for.

"Well, I assume this isn't a strictly social call. What do you need, man?"

Zach pulled into the parking lot at the police station. "I'm looking for a guy named Frank Adams. Ever heard of him?"

"Nope. He a dealer?"

"I don't think so, but I don't really know much about him. I just need to find him. Could you put out a couple feelers for me? See if anyone has any information on him?"

"Absolutely."

He debated if he should say anything about the break-in the night before. He didn't want to spread it far and wide that he hadn't been able to protect his charge, but he couldn't get info if he didn't ask. "And would you mind keeping an ear open for anyone talking about breaking into a cop's house last night?"

"Your house?"

"Yeah."

LeRoy took his time responding. "You want to tell me what's happening?"

"Not really. I just need you to have my back on this one. Let me know if you hear anything like that."

"Sure. Always." LeRoy paused for a long second. "And say hey to your sister for me."

"Samantha is out of your league, and you know it." He liked LeRoy almost as much as he liked Reese and Keaton, but a brother was obligated to protect his kid sister from anyone interested.

LeRoy chuckled. "Hey, a guy can dream, right?"

Right. A guy could dream. But where would those dreams take him? No place safe if Julie Thomas was concerned.

Zach trudged through the bull pen, wishing that he was at the mall with Julie, wishing that he could see her face alight with the flash of another memory. Wishing that memory might be the one to break this case wide open.

Ramirez met him at his desk. "Phil is still in lockup."

"Has he asked for me?"

"Not by name, but he keeps saying he knows people here and that we need to let him out."

Zach smirked. "Let's go pay the little guy a visit." Clapping Ramirez on the shoulder, he led the way toward the detention area.

When they were finally seated across the table from the handcuffed informant, Zach leaned his elbows on the Formica and pressed his hands together, pointing directly at Phil's chest. "Looks like you got into a bit of trouble last night."

Phil's muddy face dropped toward the makeshift cast around his hand. Lifting his shoulder, he shook his head and jangled his handcuffs. "Not bad. Just these—" He swore, and Zach cut him off.

"Tell me why you won't give me something on Frank Adams."

Beady eyes shifted back and forth, as though the man in question might appear in the corner of the room. Sweat popped out on Phil's forehead. "No reason really. Just don't know the guy. Never heard of him."

"Who did that to your hand?" Ramirez asked. He swung his nearly black hair off his forehead with a smirk.

"No one. I fell."

"Why are you trying to protect this guy when he's got nothing but contempt for your type?"

"My type?" With a squeak in his voice, Phil glanced back up.

Zach didn't make eye contact. He purposefully looked toward the double-sided glass and the empty room beyond. "You know. The type that will roll over on a friend. The type that will turn in anyone for a... What was it? A sleeping bag? You think you might meet some guys you've turned in on the inside?"

Phil watched them, tiny eyes wide. He worked his jaw like he was chewing gum, his teeth grinding in the silence. His nose quivered like a rat's. "You think—you think there might be some of those guys still in there?"

Ramirez shrugged. "We've got no problem finding out. How 'bout you? Want to risk it?"

Shoulder twitching, Phil looked at the ceiling and then back at his hands. "I don't want to— I mean, what do you want from me?"

"Tell us where we can find Frank Adams."

Like a dead man walking, Phil hung his head low. "Rather face the inside."

Zach's gut clenched. Who was this man that those who knew him would rather face a jail full of angry men than reveal his whereabouts?

Julie's knees just would not stay still. Pressing her hands against them as she sat in front of the television didn't do anything more than make her think about how much she didn't want to be stuck at the house. Doing nothing. Helping no one.

In her dream Lonnie had been so scared.

And she'd wanted to help, wanted to do anything but sit

on a couch and wait. But she'd been unable to reach Lonnie in time.

She couldn't fight the feeling that this moment wasn't unlike her dream.

Jumping up, Julie paced the confines of the small room. All of the curtains were closed, meant to keep her safe from prying eyes and would-be attackers. But it only served to make the walls close in around her.

Samantha had ducked out for a run but promised to be back shortly. That left only Reese to look after her, and he hadn't been out of his apartment all morning.

Suddenly the creaking door echoed through the lower floors.

Finally. He was up and around. His heavy footfalls clomped down the stairs. When he appeared, he went straight for the cold coffeepot in the kitchen. Pointing toward the wood panel covering the broken windows, he said, "You sure are some houseguest. You know a simple thank-you would suffice. No need to redecorate the whole house."

She offered an apologetic smile. Zach had definitely filled him in on the attack.

He bit back a grin as he settled in with the newspaper at the breakfast table. "Looking to add a hole in our floor, too?"

She looked down at her feet, still pacing the narrow opening at the end of the hall. "Sorry. Guess I just have some pent-up energy. Zach promised to take me to the Mall of America today, but he had to go to the station."

"Take a load off." Reese threw the business section of the paper onto the opposite side of the table. "There isn't much you can do from here, and you're stuck with me until Zach gets back. Maybe we'll get a visitor."

Her gaze shot toward the boarded windows, her stomach twisting painfully. "A visitor?"

He raised both of his eyebrows. "My girlfriend said she's going to drop by today."

She slid into the seat across from him, resting her hands on the black-and-white paper. "Girlfriend?"

"Sure. You didn't think the Jones boys were confirmed bachelors or something, did you?"

"I don't know. I just—" The full weight of what he'd said slammed into her, doubling the size of the stone in her stomach. Bending over, she hazarded a wheeze before catching her breath. "Is Zach dating someone?"

Please say no. Please say no.

Reese's laughter filled the kitchen, his shoulders shaking to an unseen rhythm. "Not for a while now. Not since he joined Homicide."

A flood of relief rolled over her, almost washing away her follow-up questions. After a beat, she risked, "Why not?"

"Maybe you should ask him that question."

"Oh." She folded her hands in her lap and clamped her lips closed. He was right. She shouldn't be prying into Zach's life. She had no right to. "I'm sorry."

A dimple appeared below Reese's morning beard. "Don't be sorry. I think he'd like to know that you care."

"Please don't tell him I was asking."

"I won't say a thing." Reese turned his attention back to the sports section, and for almost two minutes neither of them said another word. Finally he let out a little sigh. "I think Homicide is a hard job. Until you, I don't think Zach ever had a live victim. It takes its toll on a man to work those cases day in and day out. A woman would have to be pretty strong to help him through, to let him share the things he needed to and to let him keep inside the things he couldn't talk about. I think that takes a special woman, and he knows it.

"Truth is, he's never introduced any of us to a girl like that. I'm not sure he's ever met anyone like that." He looked at her until she held his gaze. "Until now."

Goose bumps exploded up her arms, and she hugged her sweatshirt even tighter around herself.

He clearly meant her.

But he was wrong.

Zach thought of her only as a stray. Like Gizmo or any of the others he'd brought home. She wasn't strong like Reese suggested. She wasn't brave and she certainly wasn't someone who fit that description.

She was a lost puppy and Zach a kind stranger.

A compassionate, strong, handsome stranger.

Heat rushed to her cheeks. She shouldn't think about him like that. She had to keep those thoughts at bay.

The back door flew open, and her face flamed even hotter as the object of her thoughts walked into the house. "Ready to go to the mall?"

Julie couldn't help but steal quick glances at Zach out of the corner of her eye as he drove them to the mall. With every passing moment of silence, a knot in her stomach grew a little tighter. Just how much of her conversation with Reese had he heard?

She shouldn't have been talking about his love life. It was none of her business.

Still…she had no trouble conjuring images of his past girlfriends, wondering what they had been like.

The silence between them, all thick and heavy, like morning fog rolling off the river and nearly as cold, left her to scrounge for anything to fill it. He didn't seem angry. Just distracted, his gaze never wavering from the white lines disappearing beneath the car.

She'd never been so happy to see a parking lot as she

was when he pulled between rows of cars, all pointed toward the monstrous building in front of her.

As he stepped out of the car, he pointed to the sign affixed to a nearby light post. "Remember what row we're in."

"Don't worry. My short-term memory is great."

He bumped his elbow into hers with a low chuckle and without pause the tension in her middle vanished.

As they walked through the open doors and stepped into the largest single entity Julie could possibly imagine, her head spun. The pure immensity of it, even at the entrance, overwhelmed her. It was surprisingly quiet for the number of people milling in and out of stores. A series of steps crisscrossed in front of them, people meandering up and down, their arms weighted with plastic bags filled with the day's deals.

Zach led the way toward the railing, which overlooked a courtyard of sorts. Rising up toward the industrial ceiling, a giant green roller coaster clacked toward the top, and as it swooped over the apex, the screams from its riders echoed until they, too, were swallowed by the sheer size of the structure.

"Want to ride it?" He nudged her.

Not even a little bit. Her stomach hurt at just the thought. "I don't think my doctor would approve."

"All right. Anything look familiar?"

It was too big to be recognizable. There were too many pieces, too many moving parts to focus on any one thing that might jostle loose a memory. All she could offer was a wide-eyed shake of her head.

"Well, then maybe we should walk around?"

Nodding, she trailed no more than two steps behind him, unable to stop her neck from rotating around and around as she tried to take in everything. As they walked past a perfume store, someone squirted something in her face, and she blinked and recoiled against the mist that burned her eyes.

Zach's hand found her elbow, gently guiding her out of the flow of traffic. She rubbed the heels of her palms against her eye sockets before blinking away the offending spray. As it cleared, the smell of pretzels and cinnamon rolls and all things fried wafted around them.

"Better?" Zach asked.

She nodded and began to assure him that she was, but her gaze fell onto a man about twenty yards away. His blond hair flipped out from under the sides of his red baseball cap. Crossing his arms over his plain white T-shirt, he leaned against the concourse railing and smirked at her, his eyes never wavering.

Chills raced down her spine, and she grabbed for Zach's hand. His long fingers wrapped around hers as worry wrinkled his forehead. "What's wrong?"

Heart in her throat, she couldn't take her gaze off the man in the baseball cap. "I—I'm not sure. But that man. He's looking at me funny. And…there's something not right."

Zach followed her gaze with his own, but the man twisted away, blending into the crowd, his menacing stare suddenly lifting. Turning back to her, Zach dipped to look right into her eyes. "Do you want to leave?"

Yes. But then she might miss her chance to find something familiar.

The baseball cap guy might just be another shopper. She'd certainly had no difficulty creating illusions in her own mind. Maybe he was just another one. With Zach at her side, nothing was going to happen.

"Let's keep walking."

So they did. For fifteen minutes they strolled, weaving through the crowd, peeking into store windows, watching the crowds in line for the amusement rides. All the while, he kept his fingers firmly entwined with hers.

And without that stabilizing force, she would have fallen to the ground when a broad shoulder slammed against her exposed arm. Crying out in surprise and pain, she jerked toward the man responsible, catching only his arrogant grin.

One that showed off a chipped front tooth.

Air vanished and the entire world froze.

Fear seized her throat, and she heaved a great, silent sob.

He'd followed her. And now that he'd found her, he was going to do what he'd failed to the night before.

"It's the guy from last night," she finally managed to cry.

THIRTEEN

Zach held his breath while the man in the red baseball cap looked over the crowd and waved toward them. A signal to an accomplice.

And then Baseball Cap reached behind his back, a flash of silver appearing in his hand. The weapon wasn't obnoxiously large or overly visible, but it was plenty big enough to bring Julie down—to finish the job that he'd started.

All conscious thought vanished, instinct and ten years of training taking over. Zach pressed his arm into his side against the service weapon in his shoulder holster. But pulling it out might only escalate the situation, and with the assailant having an unknown partner somewhere in this crowd, his only option was to get Julie to safety.

He offered her little more than a hand squeeze of warning before bolting into the oblivious crowd. He squeezed between two chattering women before tearing toward the nearest staircase, his pulse already topping the charts. The women both squealed, and then roared when Julie's pursuer did the same.

Blood rushing behind his ears muffled all the ensuing noise. The clicking of the roller coaster. The rustling of shopping bags. The laughing teenage girls.

Everything except the beating of his own heart and the thudding of Julie's footsteps behind him vanished.

He toppled into a woman and murmured a silent apology, spinning to catch a glimpse of Baseball Cap. He was just steps behind them, his hand outstretched toward the hood of Julie's sweater. Zach barreled forward, pulling her with him, keeping her close enough to feel her breath on his neck. Close enough to know she was safe. Her palm grew damp, but he only squeezed tighter, unwilling to risk even loosening it a fraction to readjust.

Not until he had found a secure place for her.

But in the moment he could focus only on the three feet in front of him. Just squeeze through the line here and dodge the cart there.

Somehow they'd made it into the open, bolting across the concourse and falling through the line for some attraction that he couldn't see. A man hollered at him to slow down, and he tried to make his heart rate follow the advice. It wasn't the physical exertion that left his head spinning and eyes burning but the fear for Julie. And still the man with the chipped tooth followed them, his presence urging Zach forward, renewing his strength, keeping his feet running. *Please, God. Help me find a safe place. A safe place. A safe place.*

Lungs screaming and arms pumping, he glanced up just in time to see their salvation. A sign announcing Mall Security pointed to a door barely ten yards away. He slammed into the silver handle, and the door burst open into a narrow hallway.

Two uniformed security guards glanced up from their seats at a desk, and Zach heaved great breaths as he pulled his badge from under his jacket. "A guy with blond hair in a red ball cap was chasing us. He had a weapon. Just on the other side of the door."

Although wide-eyed and open-mouthed, the guards jumped from their seats and rushed toward the door, yelling into their radios.

When the security guards had disappeared, Julie's shaking legs couldn't hold her any longer, and she crumpled to the ground.

Zach knelt before her, running his hands up and down her arms and neck and over her cheeks. "Are you all right?"

Tears were the only answer she could offer as she gulped in great lungfuls of air against his neck. A damp spot on his collar spread as her shoulders shook in his embrace. "I'm sorry. I was so scared."

"It's okay. You're safe now. We're still together." He swiped at an errant teardrop with his thumb, the pad callused but gentle against her cheek. Tilting her face down, he pressed his lips against her forehead.

A sob caught her off guard, and she pressed her face into his immobile shoulder. In fact, all of him seemed as steady as an oak on a windless day. How could he be so calm after such an ordeal?

"I'm sorry." Her trembling lip garbled her words. Or maybe it was the width of his shoulder, which she refused to pull herself away from.

He made gentle shushing noises as he stroked her hair. "Everything's going to be all right. I'm here. You're safe. He can't hurt you now."

"What about the man who was chasing us? He had a gu-un!"

"I know. But he didn't follow us in here. They'll look for him on security cameras." His voice dropped low. "But if a security guard on the ground doesn't find him, he's probably long gone."

Which meant he was still out there.

But she was safe. In here. Wherever *here* was.

She was safe in Zach's arms.

It wasn't until the rest of her body had stopped trembling that she realized he wasn't as unaffected as she'd assumed. His hands, too, shook from the tumult of emotions. Lacing her fingers through his uninjured hand, she leaned away far enough to look into his eyes.

Fear and longing swept across his face. A sigh lifted and lowered his shoulders. "If I knew for sure that you weren't married…" He dragged the words out, each one utter misery. A muscle in his shadowed jaw jumped.

A butterfly swooped inside her, its flight uneven and terrifying. But it carried a certainty that she couldn't pinpoint. Squeezing his hand that was still in hers, she gave him a wavering smile. "I'm not married."

"How can you be sure?"

She couldn't tell him the whole truth. If she'd felt even half the range of emotions that Zach induced in her for any other man, she'd have known it from the moment she opened her eyes in that hospital room. Closing her eyes, she let a partial truth out on a breath and a prayer. "He'd have been the first thing I remembered."

Suddenly Zach moved, bringing his face close to hers. She could smell his spicy aftershave, feel the warmth of his skin, but he stopped short of what she really wanted.

Lips tingling in anticipation, she waited, praying he'd do what they'd danced around for days.

He slipped an arm around her back, pulling her fully against him as they knelt on the unforgiving tile floor. His arm was strong, protective, his fingers soft as they caressed her jaw. His thumb dragged along the line of her lower lip, leaving a path of smoldering embers in its wake.

Her eyes burned at the tenderness of his touch. After

weeks of knowing only pain at the hands of her attacker, she could barely believe that such a strong man could be so gentle.

Finally he pressed his lips to hers, and it was everything she'd hoped for, every promise fulfilled. Head spinning and lungs exploding, she clung to him, grabbing the front of his shirt into both of her fists and holding on for everything she was worth.

She didn't have to wonder if she'd ever known a moment like this before.

No one had ever had such a perfect kiss, all affection, joy and longing.

Had anything ever been so sweet? Had her heart ever ached so acutely? Joy and pain warred within her. She couldn't stay in his arms forever, and it tore at the deepest part of her. The desire to be safe and to know the truth were nothing next to her longing to stay with him. That she was expendable, that he would soon let her go, stole what little air she had left, and she tore away from him.

"I'm sorry," he whispered. Her stomach clenched. "This wasn't the time or place for that. But I'm not sorry I kissed you. I've been wanting to do that for a while now."

Me, too.

She couldn't confess it or risk seeing the pity in his eyes, so she stared at her hands folded in her lap and nodded. "Maybe we should go. I'm supposed to see the doctor today, and maybe he'll look at your hand."

"All right." Zach reached out to take her hand, but she pushed herself to her feet without letting him touch her again. That was a recipe for pain. Keeping her distance was her only hope now.

That and finding the key to unlock her memory so she could go home.

The longer she stayed, the more danger she was in. It wasn't just her life on the line. Her heart hung in the balance, too.

Zach folded his arms across his chest as Dr. Willow, who was tall and lanky like his name suggested, flashed a light into Julie's eyes. She perched on the edge of an E.R. bed, squinting into the light.

Willow mumbled something before taking her hand and running his fingers over the bones on the back and gently rotating it. "How's that feel?"

"Fine. It's a little tender when I press too hard against it like this." She bent it back.

"That's normal. Nothing to worry about. Just give it as much rest as you can."

She nodded, and he moved back up to the scratch on her forehead, the one that had originally been a bump that rivaled Mount Rushmore, the injury that had caused the most issues.

"This is healing just fine." He ran a thumb over the red mark. "Is it sensitive to the touch?"

"No. It feels good."

"Good." He jotted something into his electronic chart. "Where'd you get the other bruise?"

Zach caught Julie's gaze as it swung to him. What would she say? He shrugged. It was entirely up to her to decide how much she wanted to reveal.

"I got in a fight."

With just a raised eyebrow, the doctor asked his unspoken question, and Julie continued, "Someone is still after me. But don't worry. I won this battle."

Zach couldn't help the little smile that worked its way across his mouth. She was something else. It was one of the things that he liked best about her. Smart and snappy.

And a great kisser.

Heat washed over him, and he pressed his lips together at the memory of holding her in his arms. She'd fit so perfectly, clinging to his comfort. Of course, he'd needed to wrap his arms around her as much as she'd needed it.

"Are you having headaches?" Willow frowned.

"Only when people slam me into walls." She was so deadpan that when she looked in Zach's direction again, the air between them sizzled with unrecognized laughter.

The good doctor didn't look like he fully believed her, but he didn't harp on the subject. Wrapping his stethoscope back around his neck, he put his hands on his hips. "How's your memory?"

"I remembered someone that I met before the attack." Her voice swung up on the last word, as though she was casting for a compliment. "And I know the words to a hymn that we sang in church."

"Good for you. Do you remember when you first sang the song or met your friend?"

The pink in her cheeks drained away as she shook her head.

Willow pulled up a rolling stool so that he no longer towered above his patient. He crossed his arms over his chest and leaned back. His graying eyebrows closed the distance above his nose until they formed only one line. "I'm not going to lead you on, Julie. I'm worried that your memory hasn't returned."

"But it's coming back. I recognized Mickey's Diner."

"And do you know when you were last there?" The doctor's tone wasn't unkind, but the true answer to his question made Zach's head throb. This wasn't good news.

She wrapped her arms around her middle, the bruise at her elbow clearly visible since she'd taken off her hoodie.

Dr. Willow eyed it, but didn't specifically ask about it.

"The mind is a strange science. Often the things that we know about it aren't really as certain as we'd like them to be. From a physical standpoint your brain is fine. The swelling was completely gone before you were released, and the rest of your injuries are healing just like I'd expect for a healthy woman of your age.

"But sometimes the mind works in ways we don't understand, trying to protect itself. Your brain may be doing that right now, trying to keep from remembering a painful part of your past." He rested his hands on his knees. "It's good that you remembered the words to a hymn. That means the memories aren't gone. They're just being protected right now. The only thing we can do is keep waiting, keep looking for things that might release what's being protected. Sometimes worrying about it only adds pressure. Try to relax, and see if that helps." Dr. Willow gave Zach a hard glare. "Try harder to keep her safe. She doesn't need more bumps."

"I'm working on it," Zach said.

Julie slid off the bed. "Thank you." She inched closer to Zach, and he stood to slip a hand behind her back. When his fingers brushed the soft cotton of her shirt, she flinched, and he dropped his hand. Was she thinking about how his arms had circled her when they kissed? He sure was.

"What happened to your hand, Detective Jones?"

Zach held up the gauze-wrapped injury. "I cut myself on a piece of glass."

"Want me to take a look at it?"

"Yes," Julie said at the same moment that he declined the offer.

She glared at him with raised eyebrows.

"Fine. But it feels all right." He held it out, and Willow unwrapped the gauze. It stung as he peeled off the butterfly bandage, revealing the open wound. The edges of the gash were pink and slightly wrinkled from the moisture of the ointment.

The doctor looked at it under the light, a slow grin falling into place. "Good work. It looks great. Did you do this yourself?"

"Julie cleaned it up. She said I didn't need stitches."

With an approving glance, Willow said, "Very nice. Ever think about being a nurse?"

"I don't know."

They all chuckled as the doctor put a new bandage in place and sent them on their way with an admonition to relax and try to stay out of harm's way.

Easy for him to say.

No one was trying to kill him for the memories that were so slow to return.

As they walked toward the exit, two nurses stepped in front of them. Julie slammed to a halt, and Zach was three steps in front of her before he realized she wasn't by his side. Spinning, he stared at her. "What's going on?"

"I think I have that shirt."

"What shirt?"

She pointed toward the blonde walking ahead of them. Her scrub top was bright blue and covered in fluffy white sheep that jumped over little fences and ate tufts of green grass.

"What do you mean?"

Julie walked to his side, her gaze never wavering from the woman, who had made it to the end of the hall. "I think I really was a nurse."

He stared at his hand that she had cared for so quickly and carefully. He should have known. She was perfect for it. So gentle yet strong. Kind but tough.

Nothing could change the things that were written on the deepest part of her heart. Her compassion. Her sweetness.

Her courage. These were the things that probably made her a fantastic nurse. They were also the qualities that made his heart rate double when she entered a room.

He risked a kiss to her cheek, her skin smooth. "I'm not surprised. I'm sure you're a great nurse."

Beaming up at him, she tucked her hand into his and followed him toward the exit.

"I'm going to send your picture to human resources departments at every hospital in the Twin Cities to see if anyone can identify you. All right?" She nodded, but the grim set of her mouth made him wonder if she was thinking the same thing he was. If she was from somewhere nearby, someone would have come forward with her name by now after all the online and print coverage by the newspaper.

In the parking lot he opened her door, waited for her to get settled and closed it behind her. Walking around the front of the car, he scanned the lot for any uninvited guests. Whoever was after her had known she was home alone the night before. He'd followed her to the mall and waited for an opportunity to strike. He was being more brazen, more bold. Why? What propelled him to be so brash? Did he know that every day she was getting closer to uncovering a memory that could identify her attacker and maybe the person who had taken the baby?

The parking lot was quiet for a Friday afternoon, only a handful of other cars coming and going. Still he memorized a few models just to keep his eyes open for them.

Sliding behind the wheel, Zach turned on the car. "Ready to go home?"

"Yes." She had pulled her knees up to her chin, hugging her legs against her chest. She let her head fall back against the seat, her eyes drooping closed.

Truthfully he was ready for a nap, too. And he hadn't

even been thumped on by the doctor. How she was still alert was something of a wonder.

As he put the car in gear, his phone rang. Putting the gear back into Park, he pulled the cell out of his pocket. The number on the screen was unfamiliar but not blocked. Maybe Phil had had a change of heart after an afternoon in the city jail.

"This is Zach."

"Detective Jones?" The voice on the other end was high-pitched and familiar, but he didn't immediately recognize it.

"Yes. Who's this?"

"Wendy Caruthers. From McNulty's Pub."

He shot a glance at Julie, whose eyes were still closed. Her shoulders rose and fell in an even rhythm. "Hi, Wendy. What can I do for you?"

"Melinda, the hostess, she's back and just came in to pick up her check. I told her you were looking for her, and she said she could stick around for half an hour. You can swing by before the dinner crowd comes in, if you want."

Perfect. He desperately needed to interview Melinda, possibly one of the last people to see Julie before the attack. He couldn't get all the way home to drop Julie off and make it downtown in time to meet Melinda before she left. But taking Julie with him to the pub wasn't an option. She needed rest and a safe place to sleep.

Hadn't the doctor said that relaxation could be just what her mind needed to unlock all of her secrets? But taking her to McNulty's could be a familiar place that had the potential to do the same.

He stared at the ceiling, praying for a divine word of wisdom.

Nothing happened.

"Are you still there?" Wendy sounded impatient, the

click of her pen against a table or her hostess stand accentuating her words.

"I'm here. I'll be there as soon as I can. Please don't let Melinda leave."

He pocketed the phone and shifted the car into Drive.

Without opening her eyes, Julie asked, "What was that about?"

"Someone who might have seen you the night of the attack."

She sat up straight, turning toward him. Her eyes bore into the side of his head as he maneuvered them toward the cross street. "Who?"

"I told you about that pub, McNulty's." She nodded. "The hostess who was working that night is back in the country and can meet me."

"Then let's go." With her brown eyes bright and her face alight with hope, she leaned toward him.

"Maybe I should drop you off at home first."

"So what can happen? So he can find me alone again? So I can sit like a bump on a log and be completely useless? Take me with you."

The bags beneath her eyes had grown, and her movements were stilted. Exhaustion was just around the corner, but she fought it with her words, her stuttering breaths seeming to boost her resolve.

"You really need to rest."

"I know. And I'll rest after I remember. Or after someone remembers me."

He couldn't argue with her sentiment, so he whipped the car toward downtown.

FOURTEEN

Julie stepped through the entrance to McNulty's as Zach held the door open for her, his eyes following her movements so closely that she took careful steps. She couldn't have him thinking she was too tired or too weak to follow through on this lead. It was their first real hope for details about that night since the video of her carrying baby Kay.

A pretty woman with a long black braid hanging over her shoulder glanced up as they entered. "Well, well, Detective Jones. You made it."

"Hi, Wendy." He motioned to his right. "This is Julie."

Wendy stepped forward and reached for Julie's hand. "I've seen your picture in the paper, but you look a whole lot better than you did with that black eye."

Straightforward and plainspoken. Julie liked her immediately. "Very nice to meet you."

"You said Melinda was here." Zach's head swung around to get a view of the entire room, which was empty save for a dozen tables, their chairs and a long wooden bar lined with matching stools.

Wendy hitched a thumb over her shoulder. "She's in the back. I'll go get her."

The weight of a gaze on her back swept over her, and Julie spun to look through the wall of small windowpanes.

Several people walked the downtown sidewalks, and a non-descript black car rolled past, but other than that, it was deserted. No one was watching her.

She just couldn't shake the feeling that they weren't alone or that someone was tracing her every movement. Perhaps it was a residual effect of being hunted and chased across the city.

"It's you!" The announcement carried across the room as a robust young woman sashayed from the kitchen door. Her broad shoulders and matching hips swayed as she drew closer to them. Her smile spoke a familiarity that Julie couldn't quite place, but it set hope loose in her chest. Maybe, just maybe, this woman could help them.

"Do you know me?"

"Of course." Hands plopped at her waist, Melinda flipped her blond hair over her shoulder with a twitch of her neck. "Don't you remember? You came in here the other night?" She snapped her fingers three times, looking toward the ceiling. "I think it was Friday night. Yeah. Definitely the Friday right before my wedding."

Julie caught Zach's gaze, and they shared a smile. "I'm afraid I don't remember being here. I had an…accident, and I'm just trying to piece together what happened that night."

"Wow." Melinda's jaw dropped, revealing a wad of chewing gum in her cheek. "You mean, I saw you that same night."

"I guess so." Julie folded her hands in front of her.

Zach stepped forward, revealing his badge and finally introducing himself. "I'm Detective Jones. I'm looking into Julie's accident. Can we ask you a few questions?"

"Sure, sure." She led the way toward a table and plopped down across from them. "What do ya wanna know?"

"Well, everything." Julie leaned her elbows on the table

and cupped her chin in her hand. "Do you remember when I came in? Was I alone?"

"'Course not. You came in because of the baby. Remember?" Julie shook her head, and Melinda giggled. "Right. I forgot." She drummed her fingers on the table, studying the wood grain for a long second. "I guess it was about nine or nine-fifteen. Our dinner customers were just clearing out and Bob had been at the piano for like half an hour. He usually gets here at eight, but I remember that he was late and some of the regulars were mad that he wasn't here.

"Anyway, we were pretty busy. It was really cold that night, and everyone coming in was ordering hot drinks just to warm themselves up. I even had a cup of coffee at the stand just to warm my hands when some idiot left the door open too long."

Great. But none of it mattered. Julie needed to know about Lonnie and Kay, not the early spring weather. "So when did I come in?"

"When I invited you in. I saw you out the window. You were out there for like twenty minutes." She chewed on her gum as though she'd never tasted anything so fascinating in her life, pressing it against the tip of her tongue before blowing a bubble. "And the baby was crying 'cause it was cold. So I told you you could sit inside while you waited. You stayed on the end of that bench by the front door, staring out the window the whole time."

Zach took in a sharp breath and let it out more slowly. "Any idea who she was waiting for?"

"Nope. She just sat and rocked that little munchkin. We got real busy after that, and I didn't pay much attention to her. Then about ten, when Bob went on his second break, there was a fight at the bar. Someone was ticked off, and I looked at you and the kid to make sure you were okay. You were checking your phone."

"What kind of phone? Did she call anyone?" Zach's interruption flew out so fast that Melinda sat back with a grin on her face.

"I don't know. It was a smartphone of some kind. But best as I could tell, she was just looking for something on it. Maybe like an address or something. I thought I saw a map on it, but I just got a peek. Nothing big."

"How long did I stay?"

Melinda let her ear drop to her shoulder and stared up at the ceiling. "Not much longer after that. You got up and said thanks for letting you stay inside and then you left."

"Alone?" Zach's voice was gruff. He wasn't getting the clues he wanted, either. "Did anyone follow her?"

"Not from in here. But I noticed this tall guy, dark hair, walking down the street behind them. I couldn't see his face so much, but he was kind of skinny and wore a big coat."

Tall, dark and skinny. Julie's stomach churned and sweat broke out on the palms of her hands. The descriptors fit Frank Adams—and a million other guys in the city. But still. Could it have been him? Had Serena and Josh been right? Was he following her that night?

"What direction did they go in?" Zach was literally on the edge of his seat, hope carrying his voice.

Melinda pointed toward the door and twisted her wrist. "Toward the park."

Fear tiptoed down Julie's back, and she shivered at its freezing touch. Whoever that man was, he was probably the last to see her and the last to see Kay before she disappeared.

They had to find him.

The next morning Zach looked up from reading an email from Ramirez about Frank Adams just as Reese stumbled into the kitchen. He made a beeline for the coffeepot, filling a mug to the brim and then touching it to his lips. He winced and jerked back, blowing on it before trying again.

"Late night?" Zach asked.

"Stupid stakeout. The guy hasn't moved a muscle in three weeks. I don't know what the captain thinks is going to happen, but I sure know that I'm going to retire long before it does."

Julie turned from her place at the stove, a colorful apron covering her regular jeans and T-shirt. "Will a pancake help?"

Reese shook his head slowly. "*A* pancake will not help." Her smile disappeared, replaced by a look of complete loss. "But three might do the trick."

And just like that, she was practically dancing through the kitchen, setting a plate and silverware on the table, flipping pancakes like an expert and twirling to a tune that only she could hear.

"What's gotten into her?" Reese asked, jabbing his fork in Julie's direction.

Good question, and one Zach couldn't answer. But, boy, he'd like to have this version of Julie around for a long time. What would it be like to share a pot of coffee every morning and a bowl of ice cream every night? What would it be like to share a life of normal things—not this frantic, frazzled uncertainty?

His chest nearly glowed at the idea, warmth radiating down his arms and leaving him nearly as satisfied as the pancakes she'd served him ten minutes before.

When she arrived at the table with three flapjacks stacked on her turner, she plopped them down on Reese's plate. He slathered them in syrup before cutting them in long strips one direction, turning his plate and cutting the opposite angle. Stabbing his fork through a three-stack, he brought them to his mouth, devouring them. He shoveled the rest of his breakfast into his mouth faster than Zach could blink.

Julie laughed and put her hand on Reese's shoulder. "Were you hungry?"

"I guess so." He raised his eyebrow and rubbed his belly. "But I could probably make room for at least two more. They're just that good."

"Oh, you are a sweet-talker." She giggled and playfully slapped his arm. But she did just what he wanted, walking back to the stove and pouring two more perfect circles onto the griddle.

Something hot and angry flashed through Zach's chest. It stung like heartburn, only lower and madder. It roared its disapproval of this interaction, of the closeness that Julie and Reese shared.

He chugged the last of the orange juice that Julie had poured him—the entire breakfast in appreciation for his kindness, for giving her a place to stay.

Truth was, he liked having her around way more than he should.

He wasn't a geek passed over for the star quarterback by the prettiest girl in school. He wasn't even a freshman passed over for his senior brother—although that had actually happened a time or two.

She wasn't his to long for.

She belonged somewhere else. And when he found that place, he was going to have to give her back. Maybe it was only a couple hundred miles away. Or maybe it was on the other side of the country. Wherever she belonged, it wasn't here. It wasn't with him.

At just the thought his stomach threatened to revolt against the pancakes he'd just eaten.

He took a sip of coffee as Julie delivered another stack.

She leaned on Reese's shoulder as he pointed out something in the newspaper. "Have you seen this?" his brother asked.

"What?" She leaned in even closer, her chin nearly even with his.

The rest of their conversation disappeared behind the thunder in Zach's ears, and no amount of calmly drinking his coffee or checking emails from work was going to make it go away.

Jerking away from the table, he stalked toward the back door, yanked it open and marched onto the back patio.

The morning was fresh and clean and he inhaled great gulps of the crisp air, letting it wash the tension from his soul.

What was wrong with him?

First he couldn't stop thinking about her, then he'd kissed her. And now he was jealous of his own brother, who was about to propose to his own girlfriend.

Zach scrubbed a hand down his face then ruffled his hair, all the while pacing the confines of the back porch.

Finally he sank into a patio chair, pressing his elbows against his knees, resting his chin in his hands and staring at the cloudless blue sky. Morning birds chirped, but he could find no joy in their song.

God, what has happened to me? Have I royally messed up this entire case?

Julie was supposed to be just that, a case. He'd wanted to help her out, give a victim a temporary home.

So why did it feel like she'd found a more permanent one in his heart?

He'd always been a "feetfirst, first time" kind of guy. Jump in carefully, make sure the waters were safe and clear of hazards. Perhaps he'd started that way with Julie, but somewhere between pulling her out of the river and realizing she was in danger at the mall, he'd tossed caution out the window and let himself fall hard into the churning waters.

But what did he hope was going to happen? He had no endgame in this situation. It could only wind up hurting him and her if he moved in closer. If he let himself stay attached. If he kissed her again.

And boy did he want to kiss her again.

"Did my pancakes not sit well with you?"

He jolted in Julie's direction, her voice ripping him from his silent prayers. "No. Not at all. I—I just needed some fresh air."

He didn't like craning his neck to look into her face, so he rose, forcing her to tilt her head to get a good look at him. "Is everything all right? You looked…upset in there." She clearly chose her words carefully. One more thing he liked about her.

"Just thinking about your case." *And wishing you didn't have to leave when it's solved.*

She nodded, hanging her head and staring at the ground like she was going to count every single blade of grass. "Any idea where Frank Adams is?"

"Not yet. But I have a few friends looking into it. And Ramirez emailed me this morning that he thinks he's found a local connection. But he hasn't unearthed anything about a missing baby. It's like she's absolutely vanished."

"What else are you thinking about?" She reached for his hand, her fingers just brushing the side. It took every ounce of strength in him not to react, not to twine their fingers together and pull her to his chest.

You.

He wanted to say it aloud, to admit that she'd been taking up way more space in his mind than he'd given her permission to.

At that moment Gizmo bounded up to them, bumping

his head against their hands, begging to be patted. Zach took the opportunity to pull his hand away, rubbing the shaggy mutt behind the ears until he howled with joy and licked Zach's hand.

Pain flickered in Julie's eyes, the brown there shifting into something that didn't look far from heartbreak. He couldn't look at it for longer than a second, as it tore at his core. She plastered a smile into place, but the quiver of her chin didn't lie.

Being apart from her family—from her memories—was breaking her down, tearing her to pieces. She'd told him when she first arrived in his home that she missed her family. She carried around a hollow place that the love for them had once filled.

If he couldn't keep his own heart from breaking, he surely could help hers not to.

As if on cue, his phone rang. It was LeRoy. "I need to take this."

"Sure." She pantomimed going back inside, and he nodded as he pressed the button to answer the call.

"LeRoy. Tell me you've got something for me."

"Hey, man. I've got some good news."

Hope raced through his chest like a kid in a soapbox derby. "You found Frank?"

"Not exactly." Something crashed on the other end of the line and LeRoy hollered at someone to clean it up.

"Don't leave me hanging." It took a concentrated effort to keep his voice from carrying a note of exasperation. "What's going on? What do you know?"

"Sorry about that. There's a guy that's been staying here the last few nights. He's done some bad stuff, but he's trying to get clean. Anyway, he told me last night that he worked with a guy named Frank on some petty theft stuff a couple years back. He knows where Frank's hideout is."

"Where is it?"

Zach could almost see LeRoy rubbing his bald head in the silence. "Well, that's the thing. He won't tell me, and he says he won't talk to you over the phone. He'll only meet with you in person and if you promise that he won't be arrested for that theft."

He didn't have the authority to make any such promise. Especially on a likely misdemeanor where the statute of limitations may have already run out. But the perp didn't know that. And Zach sure wasn't going to lose out on his only real lead in weeks because of it.

"Set it up. I'll be at Oasis in forty-five minutes."

"Will do."

He pocketed his phone and dashed for the house, Gizmo following close at his heels. Inside, Julie stood at the sink in the otherwise empty room.

"Where's Reese?"

She looked up from the sudsy water. "He was tired, so he went back to bed for a while." She looked at him hard, as if she were trying to read his mind. "Why? What's going on?"

"I had a break in the case."

"My case?"

He grinned. "Yes. Yours. But I need to go meet with a guy who might be able to tell us how to find Frank Adams."

"Can I come with you?"

"No." It was out before he had really given it any thought. But she couldn't go with him. It wasn't safe for her there. He had no idea what to expect, and he wasn't about to put her in the line of potential danger just because she didn't want to stay behind.

Her hands splashed into the water, her face falling right along with them. "Okay."

"Listen, it's not safe for you there."

"And it is for you?"

He laughed at her innocent question. "Julie, I'm armed and trained."

"Right." She looked away, so he tilted her head back in his direction.

"You'll be safe here." Mouth hanging open, his words stopped as a sickening feeling filled his gut. Her safety within the house wasn't guaranteed anymore. Whoever had attacked her had done so in this very room. Maybe he should find somewhere else for her to stay until things were wrapped up. They were close to cracking the case. They had to be. And until then…well, he'd get creative. "Actually, maybe I'll ask Reese to take you over to Rosie's apartment."

"Rosie?"

"His girlfriend. You'll like her. And then you'll be out of the house."

Her eyes flashed with understanding. He knew she knew that he wasn't afraid of her going stir-crazy locked inside the house. He was afraid of unwelcome visitors again. But Rosie was almost certainly an unknown factor to the men after Julie. She should be safe with Reese and Rosie until he could track down Frank.

"All right?"

"Yes." She chewed on her bottom lip. "But you be careful, too."

"No worries."

Without thinking about it, he pressed a quick kiss to her upturned lips, the sweet normalcy of it almost bowling him over. Her wet hands found his shirt, but he didn't even mind the water dripping down his front as she nestled against him.

First he had to find Frank, and then he had to figure out what he was going to do about this woman who took his breath away.

He raced upstairs, pounded on Reese's door and waited

until Reese confirmed he was up before asking him to watch over Julie and take her to Rosie's, to a safe place. After getting Reese's agreement, Zach grabbed his keys, waved goodbye to Julie and pulled the locked door closed behind him.

The street was silent, save for a jogger running with her dog as he slipped behind the wheel and zipped toward LeRoy's place.

Lord, let him find Frank Adams.

Julie glanced at Reese as he paused at yet another stop sign, the floorboard of his little pickup rattling to the rhythm of the song on the radio. She played with the frayed edge of a tear in the fabric of the bench seat, leaning into the motion of the truck, as though she might help it rattle down the pavement.

Reese hadn't said much since she'd put out a fresh dish of water for Gizmo and followed Reese out of the house. He'd opened her car door and closed it behind her. He'd turned the key in the ignition and swiped at the knob on the radio that instantly blasted.

But he hadn't said anything.

She'd opened her mouth to ask him what was going on. More than once.

Every time she bit her tongue and waited for him to speak first. His gaze was somewhere far away, somewhere with someone other than her. And if she were completely honest, she wished she was with someone else, too.

Zach had said it wasn't safe, had said she should hide out with Reese and Rosie. It was safer for her to be there. She *knew* that. Yet she didn't *feel* safer. Her chest burned with the desire to be where Zach was.

"You'll like Rosie."

Reese's quiet words surprised her, and Julie turned to

fully watch his expression. It was tight, pained. "I'm sure I will." The easygoing, jovial man who had spilled the beans about Zach's love life was gone. Worry creased his brow. "But you don't want to take me there."

He blinked, stopping again at a residential intersection. Settling his gaze on the point where his hands rested at the top of the steering wheel, he shook his head. "I want you to be safe."

"And…you want Rosie to be safe, too."

"Yes."

A clamp around her heart yanked tight. Of course. Danger followed her wherever she went, and Reese would do anything to keep Rosie from ending up near that.

"I'm sorry." She pressed her palm to his arm as he released the brake, and the truck rolled into the cross street. "We can go—"

Her words vanished beneath a deafening explosion, the force of the impact slamming her into the passenger door and stealing her breath. Her head smacked the window, releasing a high-pitched ringing in her ears. Her teeth caught the inside of her cheek, and the acrid taste of blood filled her mouth.

She shook her head to clear the fog, catching only a glimpse of the white van that had plowed into the side of the truck and Reese's limp form crumpled against the steering wheel before her own door was wrenched open. A disembodied hand held a knife that sliced her seat belt; another arm circled her chest and pulled her from the confines of the cab.

"Help him." She tried to point toward Reese, but the arm dragged her across the asphalt. Pulling on the slippery sleeve of a windbreaker jacket, she tried to regain her breath and clear her mind. Everything was happening so fast.

"Shut up, or I'll kill you, too." His breath was hot and wet against her ear, his words sliding like a cold hand around her heart.

They'd found her. They'd followed and stalked her.

And they'd killed Reese to get to her.

Julie screamed and kicked, searching for some sort of leverage to fight back, but the cracked pavement did little but bump under her heels as her captor dragged her toward the van.

Reaching over her shoulder with her only free hand, she clawed at his face. He grunted and swore when her fingernail caught his cheek, but his grip around her chest pinning her arm to her side never loosened.

"Let me go!"

"Shut up," he growled, shoving something that tasted like moldy cheese into her mouth. She gagged and wiggled, sobbed and writhed. He never let go.

And then the van's sliding back door flew open, its rumble loud in light of her muted cries.

This couldn't be it. This couldn't be the end.

He shoved her into the bay area, where all the seats had been stripped out. She bounced across the unforgiving floor, slamming into the far wall as the door closed.

Another figure hovered over her, all broad shoulders and wide stance, despite his bent posture under the low ceiling.

"Well, well, well. You just won't die, will you, Miss Bullock?"

She blinked frantically in the direction of the voice, trying to identify her new captor and make sense of the name he called her. But she didn't have time to dwell on it as the van started with a telltale rumble and pulled into traffic.

Where were they taking her? She tried to voice the question, but it was stopped by the rag still in her mouth, and she reached a sore arm up to pull it out.

"What do you want? Who are you?"

The driver squealed his tires as he maneuvered the van out of the neighborhood and away from whoever might have witnessed the accident. On an adjacent street the sun shone through the windshield, illuminating her abductor's sneering face. She'd seen it twice before in pictures and once in person. All angular planes, angry eyes and crooked nose. And that unmistakable red scar from his lip to his chin.

Her head burned as a memory flashed before her. Surrounded by trees, he'd hit her, and she'd fallen. And he'd taken baby Kay right out of her arms.

God have mercy on her, for Frank Adams certainly would not.

FIFTEEN

Zach swung his car door open, halfway out before the sedan was fully stopped. Slamming it closed behind him, he ran up the front walkway, nodding to a couple of men as they exited through the front door.

Slipping inside, he headed straight for LeRoy's office, entering through the glass door without even knocking.

His friend looked up at the unannounced intrusion. "You didn't waste any time getting here, did you, Jones?"

"I'm on a deadline. So where's your guy?"

"Dunn. He's just down the hall. I'll go get him." Zach made a move to follow the shelter's director out into the hallway, but stopped when LeRoy held up a hand. "Maybe you better wait here. You're about as cool as a fish frying over a campfire."

Zach clapped his twitching hands together and nodded. "Let's make this quick. I've got a perp to find." *And a girl to save.*

LeRoy didn't need to know that last part.

The phone in his pocket vibrated against his leg, and he snatched it out and to his ear without even checking to see who was calling.

"Zach." His brother's voice was strained, pained.

"Reese? What's wrong?"

"They took her." Reese's words weren't much more than a breath, nearly disappearing below a din of sirens and voices.

Zach knew that sound. It was unmistakably a crime scene. A lump rose in his throat so big that he couldn't even croak out a follow-up question.

"Was taking Julie to…Rosie's." He panted between words but pushed on. "White van crashed into my truck. They took her."

All the oxygen in the room vanished. Zach gasped, leaning against a wall the only way to stay on his feet. "Are you injured?"

"Not bad. Hit my head on the steering wheel, but when I came to, I was just bruised up."

"You see what direction they went?"

"No." Zach hung up the phone and slammed his fist against the wall, the pain deep within needing an exit. It only made his hand burn, but he did it again, connecting with the cinder block and managing to do nothing more than scrape his knuckles.

Dear God, I've lost her. Help me find her. Please, help me find her.

The office door swung open, and LeRoy led a short guy in baggy jeans into the office. "This is Dunn."

Stepping into the man's personal space, Zach glared at him hard. "Tell me where I can find Frank Adams right now."

The guy shuffled back a couple steps, tossing his hair out of his eyes. "That's pricey info. What are you going to give me for it?"

In a flash Zach had the man pressed against the opposite wall, his fists holding on to Dunn's shirt. "Tell. Me. Where. Adams. Is."

The thug flinched and tried to disappear into the wall at

his back, but there was nowhere to go. "I don't know. I just worked some jobs with him three years ago. I don't know. But I might remember if you'll promise me that I won't be charged for those thefts."

"Do I look like I'm in the mood to barter?" He flexed his arms, which were shaking with the tension still charging through him. "You want me to throw in conspiracy to kidnap and attempted murder to your rap sheet? Tell me. Everything."

LeRoy stepped to their side, laying a hand on Zach's shoulder, when Dunn flashed him a look of fear. "Whoa. Zach, what's going on, man?"

Without taking his eyes off the informant, he said, "Adams has her."

"Who?" LeRoy was genuinely flummoxed, but he dropped his hand, probably fearing that he'd lose it if he didn't move it.

"The girl I'm falling for."

Wow. That came out of nowhere, but it sure rang true. And it explained the ache in his heart, the one that had settled in the moment Reese had said she'd been taken. This was so much more than protective instincts. It went beyond a simple attraction. In the face of unspeakable danger, she'd displayed her true heart.

And that's what he was falling for.

But he couldn't do a thing about it until he saved her life.

Dunn was doing a pretty good fish impression, mouth opening and closing without making a noise, so Zach gave him a little shake.

"Talk."

"Back then…um…thr-three years ago, Frank used to stash some of the high-end merchandise at his place outside town."

"Where? He doesn't have any property registered in his name."

Dunn shook, his hair flapping with the intensity. "It was his m-mom's place."

"Where is it? Exactly."

"Off the highway. Over near the Winchester Bridge."

Right where Samantha and Julie had been run off the road. They'd unknowingly driven right into the hornet's nest.

"Would he be out there now?"

"I don't know. Maybe." Dunn looked to LeRoy for help, but his friend held up his hands and backed off. Good man. "Last I heard he was looking for some chick who couldn't remember anything."

Zach's breaths came slow and deliberate as he got so close he could smell Dunn's bad breath. "He find her?"

"Man, I don't know. She was staying with some cop."

Zach released his grip on Dunn's shirt so fast that the other man sagged against the wall all the way to the floor.

"What's your problem?"

Jabbing a finger in Dunn's face, Zach leaned over him. "You better be right, or Frank Adams is going to be the least of your worries. Got that?"

Flying out of the shelter and into the setting sun, he slid into his car already dialing Ramirez.

"What's up?"

Zach pulled a one-eighty in the parking lot, flooring it for the very far north side of town. Too far away for any degree of comfort. There was no telling what Adams could do in the time it would take him to get there.

"Ramirez, I need a favor."

"Sure. What's up?"

He steeled himself to say the words aloud, knowing that

speaking them would make his guts burn like he'd been branded. "Julie's been kidnapped."

A hiss of understanding carried to his ear. "Is it Frank?"

"That's my best guess. He's got some chutzpah to attack her at a cop's house, and everyone we've talked to is scared stiff of this guy. You have any better ideas?"

"Nope. You know where he is?"

"I think he might be staying at a farm by Winchester Bridge that his mom owns. Can you find me an exact address?"

"You got her name?"

"No."

The keys on the cop's computer were already clicking. "I'll find it. What else?"

All of the might-bes and possible endings to the day flashed before him. What would he do if he lost Julie? Anything that he'd let himself wish for would vanish. Every dream that had snuck into his mind was on the line.

And he was going to fight with all he was worth to save them.

To save her.

"Call for some backup to meet me there. I'm going to need it."

As the van barreled down the road, Julie scrambled toward the back of the bay, pushing on the swinging doors, praying that they would open.

Frank squatted near the handle to the sliding door and only laughed at her attempts. "How stupid do you think I am?"

He didn't really want to hear her answer, so she clamped her mouth shut and cowered in the corner. A flash crossed her mind, a memory. Frank had followed her to the park. She remembered the sensation of being followed. She'd felt his presence on that night, and she'd begun running, careful not to jostle the baby in her arms.

And then he had been on her, shoving her to the ground and raising a tire iron over his head. She'd cowered then, too. And it had done nothing but allow Kay to be taken from her.

"What happened to the baby?" Her voice was surprisingly clear in spite of the tremors in her hands and tears pooling in her eyes. "What did you do with her?"

"That's not your concern." He inspected his fingernails, clearly bored with her.

"But what about her mom? Where's Lonnie? Where's the baby?"

He flipped a hand dismissively. "Again. It doesn't matter. You're not going to live long enough to see them again anyway."

So they were alive? *Please, God, let them both be alive.*

She clung to that hope, drawing strength from it and facing down her captor with a renewed fire. He might want to kill her, but he hadn't hurt Kay. At least not yet. Maybe she could get him to reveal her whereabouts. He was arrogant. And pride could almost always be stirred up into something more useful—boasting.

"I don't think you have it in you to kill me, or you would have done it already." *Good Lord, please don't let me be making the worst—and last—mistake of my life.*

He made a smug snort and just shook his head. "Ah, but it's messy, messy to clean up in a van. It's a lot easier to make a body disappear on a big ol' farm with lots of acres. And no one's looking for you anyway, are they? Emma, is it?"

Emma.

Her name was Emma. Emma Bullock.

It both stole her breath and gave her wings. How could

she have forgotten? Her mom and dad had named her after her grandmother—Emma Jean.

And Lonnie had used it so many times that Friday night. "Emma, take care of my baby. Please. Just for a little while. Don't let them take her. Okay?" Lonnie's eyes were huge and filled with fear, her voice cracking. "Emma, promise me you'll take care of her. I want her to be happy. To be safe. Keep her safe, Emma."

Emma had failed because of the man now hunched across from her.

"How did you know my name?"

"You're not very smart, are you?" He pouted a thin lower lip, his voice filled with condescension. "Where do you think your purse went?"

Of course. He'd taken her ID, her entire identity actually. He'd stolen it when he'd taken Kay. When he'd left her in the park. When he'd tried to kill her the first time.

And now he was going to try to do it again.

Zach's face flashed before her mind. She'd come so close to loving him, even if he didn't think of her the same way. Oh, she'd been afraid to love him, to show him that she cared. What could she offer him without a past?

Except a future.

Why had she been so foolish? She'd missed maybe her only chance to tell Zach that what she felt for him went so far beyond just protector or rescuer. If Frank had forcefully stolen her memories, then she'd willingly given Zach her heart.

He just didn't know that he was in possession of it. And maybe he didn't feel the same.

But the way he'd kissed her! The emotion and power in that kiss couldn't be denied. There was something there. Something between them.

And if he didn't come for her again, didn't rescue her

again, then she'd never again know another kiss so perfect, so powerful.

She'd never know anything again.

The van lumbered to a stop, gravel crunching beneath its tires and old brakes groaning.

"Get up."

She didn't move.

Frank kicked her foot, and pain shot up her leg. "I said, 'Get up.'"

Doing as she was told, she rose to her knees and followed Frank's pointing finger as he slid outside. When her feet hit the ground, she did a quick survey of the surrounding area. A long, tree-lined lane presumably led to a main road, which was too far away for her to see. Could she run the distance if she needed to? Or would hiding in the wooded area beyond the trees be a better idea?

Whipping her head around, she took in a dilapidated old farmhouse and a just as run-down barn behind it. The barn's red paint had long ago been stripped away by winds and harsh Midwest winters. All that was left of the color was a patch under a protective eave, which rattled every time the wind blew. The barn's door hung on rusted hinges that threatened to give way without notice.

God, I don't want to die here.

A dark blanket unrolled across the sky and thunder cracked in the distance.

Frank and the driver, whom he'd called Grady, both looked up at the commotion, and she took her only chance to bolt. Feet flying like she'd never moved before, she shot away from her captors, heading straight for the tree line. The wind blowing through her hair smelled of the coming rain and freedom.

But she'd only made it a few yards when a thump against her back sent her sailing to the ground. The wind blew out of her as she landed hard against the uneven dirt, her chin hitting a tree root and clapping her jaw closed. The top of her head seemed to explode with the pain, but she ignored it. Writhing and kicking, she fought for her freedom.

She tried to turn herself over for a better angle to struggle against whoever had pushed her down, but he had a knee pressed to her back. His substantial weight subdued all her attempts to break away.

"Stop moving." It was Grady on top of her.

I would if you'd get off me. The words wouldn't come, and they fused together with the flashing spots in the corners of her eyes.

Was this how she was going to die? Suffocated by an angry flunky?

"Get her inside." Frank's growl was impatient at best. It held an underlying malice that said he was looking forward to killing her.

Grady grabbed her arm, yanking her to her feet.

She gulped at the air, drinking in the sweet relief after so long without it.

Her joy was short-lived, as Grady jerked her off balance and dragged her toward the house. She dug her toes into the gravel, but it shifted, releasing her far too easily into his sinister hands. That didn't slow him down, so she ran to keep up with him and tried a different tactic. At his side, she kicked his ankle.

He stumbled and swore but didn't loosen his grip. When he righted himself, he glared at her before bringing the hand that wasn't wrapped around her arm across her cheek. Fire lit every inch of her face from her ear to her nose, and tears welled in her eyes as he hauled her toward the front door of the house.

"Not in there." Frank's tone bespoke Grady's stupidity. "Unless you want to clean up the mess."

Grady paused. He looked down at her like she wasn't worth it, then tossed her toward the barn as if she was no more than a rag doll.

Bile rose in her throat, and she heaved uncontrollably. What had she done to deserve this but be in the wrong place at the wrong time? What had she done but watch a baby for someone who needed help?

Lonnie and Kay. Wherever they were, she hoped that God would protect them because she could do nothing else.

Her feet left a trail through the straw-covered barn floor until Grady shoved her into a wooden chair. It creaked under her weight and the rough treatment. She tried to rouse some sort of retaliation out of her body when Frank handed Grady a ball of twine, which he used to secure her to the chair.

"Go get the tarp," Frank ordered. Grady grumbled but complied, sulking away.

In her bumbling brain, which searched for any memory it could materialize, something poked at her consciousness. Something was out of place. She had to figure it out before Grady returned. Grady.

He wasn't the man who had attacked her before. "Where's the blond guy, the one you sent to the mall and to the house?"

Frank frowned and rubbed his palms together in a slow, ominous motion. "Oh, we had a...parting of ways. Seems he didn't want to do anything more than scare you. But you and I both know that's not going to be enough, is it?"

A cold sweat washed over her. She had nothing left to say, no energy left to fight as Frank's wicked grin split his face.

"This'll all be over soon."

It was true what everyone said. At the end of her life, she

regretted only the things she hadn't done. Only the words she hadn't spoken.

Her early years were still hazy; she hadn't been able to fully recall her life before the attack, but without a doubt, her biggest regret was Zach. She should have told him how she felt. She should have given him a reason to tell her the same.

Now, if God didn't intervene, she'd never be able to.

A late-night freeze the day before had left the rural roads beyond Winchester Bridge slick and slushy, and Zach turned into the skid as his car fishtailed at seventy miles an hour. All of his training told him to slow down, that he couldn't help Julie if he didn't make it to her because of an accident.

His heart told him to hurry up.

If he was too late to save her, he'd never forgive himself.

"Jones, you there?" A voice from dispatch crackled over his radio rather than through his cell, and he clicked the receiver to respond.

"I'm here."

"Ramirez says that your backup is on the way. ETA seven minutes."

As he slipped across the double yellow line and eased the car back into the correct lane, he calculated the distance. His backup was going to be at least five minutes behind him. And he couldn't wait.

"Ten-four."

Asphalt disappeared beneath his tires as he flew toward the farm that was supposed to be only a couple hundred more yards away. Trees blocked his view of anything beyond the ditch, and he had to slow down or risk missing his turn.

Just in time, he saw the clearing and pulled off to the

side of the road. But he wouldn't risk alerting anyone to his presence by actually driving down the lane. He jumped out of his car and popped the trunk. Pulling out his blue, Kevlar vest, he shrugged into it before replacing his coat and zipping it up to his chin.

He checked the ammunition in his service weapon and put an extra magazine in his pocket.

God help them all if he had to use any of the bullets.

But he'd do whatever it took to protect Julie and find Lonnie and her baby. Just, please, let them still be alive. Closing the trunk lid with a soft click, he rested both hands on the edge and shut his eyes, sending up a prayer for strength and wisdom beyond anything he could muster on his own.

The dark clouds split open for a moment revealing only the edge of the sun, which still peeked above the horizon line, the entire landscape painted in stunning strokes of pink and orange for the briefest moment.

Any other day, he'd have paused to take in the beauty, taken a picture if he could. Today it just felt unfair. How could something so pretty happen on such an ugly day?

Pushing all thoughts out of his mind, he hurried into the ditch, sloshed through a muddy mess and emerged at the base of the tree line. Weapon at the ready, he let out a slow breath before setting out at a dead run. Every half dozen trees or so, he paused. Leaning against the rough bark of a pine, he closed his eyes and listened for any noise.

All was silent, save the call of the whip-poor-will.

Taking a breath, he moved to pass six more trees. A vibration in his pocket stopped him short.

Pressing the phone to his ear, he offered a simple grunt in greeting.

"It's Reese. My partner and I are on the far side of the lane opposite you."

Zach spun from his cover just enough to make out two forms in shadows on the other side of the driveway. One of them raised his hand, and Zach let out a low sigh, releasing a bit of tension with it. "I'm glad to see you, man. Are you sure you're up for this?"

"I wouldn't miss it."

The fear that had nearly choked him at Reese's call that afternoon warred with the gratitude that his brother had shown up just when he needed him. Relief outweighed the previous fear, and he shot Reese a half smile—even though there was no way he could see it. "Wearing your vest?"

"Absolutely."

Zach shot a glance at them across the road and pointed toward the end of the lane, where he assumed they'd find the house that Dunn had told him about. "You ready?"

"See you up there."

Tucking his phone away, he jogged toward the house, keeping his steps as silent as the pair opposite him. Two hundred yards from the crossroad, the lane turned at almost a ninety-degree angle, and the old house appeared like a mirage in the desert. Its windows were black, its door flimsy, but he had never been so happy to see a building in his life.

"Windows." He mouthed the word to his brother, who had drawn closer as the trees angled toward the small clearing.

Reese nodded, motioned to his partner and hustled to the front window on the far side. Zach followed suit, cupping his hands around his eyes and staring into the house, which looked as empty as a swimming hole in December.

Just then a scream split the air and lightning zigzagged across the sky.

"Julie." Her whispered name was a prayer for safety, a prayer of hope, as he dashed toward the towering barn behind the house.

The frame of the door was outlined in white light and a solid thump seemed to rattle the whole building as he reached the door.

Reese had his hand on the sliding door, prepared to open it, his partner standing by with his gun in hand.

"Ready?" Zach asked in a hushed tone that seemed distinctly at odds with his position.

Reese nodded. "You?"

Zach nodded. His insides disagreed, flipping and gurgling, but he didn't have more time to prepare for what was beyond that door. "On three."

His brother agreed, and Zach ticked off his fingers. One. Two.

Three.

SIXTEEN

Emma jerked hard to the side as the back of Frank's hand connected with her cheek again.

"I asked you a question!"

"I know." She spit at him, but her mouth was so dry that nothing came out. "I'm still not going to answer it."

He pressed his nose so close that it was almost touching hers. "Who did you tell about the kid?"

"You tell me where she is first." She rocked back and forth on the chair, which groaned under her weight, but the twine still hadn't let go.

Frank lifted his hand for another swipe at her face, but Grady grabbed his arm. "Stop it, man. She's not going to tell you anything else. Let's just do this and be done."

The murder in Frank's eyes shifted to his partner just as the barn doors flew open, groaning with the effort it took for them to move quickly. Three men with guns drawn filled the opening. Somehow her mind registered that Reese was one of them—alive and well—but she couldn't really focus on anyone other than Zach, whose eyes never wavered from Frank.

Grady dropped to his knees, holding his hands high above his head, and one of the other men stepped forward to handcuff him.

But Frank wasn't interested in an easy resolution. He ducked behind her chair, and suddenly all muzzles pointed in her direction.

Her throat felt like the Sahara as she swallowed, her gaze focused on the three guns pointing directly at her. The fourth in the room poked her in the ribs, and she flinched as far away as she could while tied to a chair.

"I wouldn't move if I were you," Frank growled low, his words directed at the man he perceived as the greatest threat.

Zach.

She tried to tell Zach to do what Frank had said. She tried to tell him to be careful. But her swollen tongue stuck to the roof of her mouth, and her words felt like gelatin, unformed and shaky.

"Drop your weapon. You're outnumbered. This won't end well for you, Adams." Zach sounded so confident, so certain, and she tried to borrow some of his strength. She just needed a word of assurance from him, but he didn't even look in her direction.

Something cool and hard pressed against her arm, and Frank yanked it up. For a moment, she thought he'd cut her, but then the bonds holding her in place fell away. She was free for only a moment as Frank's arm wrapped around her shoulders, the hunting knife in his hand dangerously close to her face. With his other hand, he prodded her back with his gun.

"I'm thinking this is going to end worse for you than for me," Frank said, a low-level chuckle coming from his throat. "You don't have anything I want."

Zach matched the other man's laugh. "Oh, I know exactly what you want. You want to know who knows about the baby."

Frank's grip tightened, and she wheezed out a breath,

scratching at his arm around her neck. "How do you know about the kid?"

"Come on, man." He tipped his chin toward Emma. "Do you think she's been staying with me for weeks and didn't tell me?"

Letting out a sigh, Frank took a step back, his hold around her letting up just enough for her to swing an elbow into the center of his stomach. His air came out in a whoosh, and she dropped to the ground as a gunshot exploded.

Frank jerked back like someone had grabbed his shoulder, firing his handgun once before falling to the ground.

The silence after the gunshots was deafening.

Everything moved in slow motion. Zach fell to his back, clutching at his chest. Emma tried to reach him, but her muscles felt like she'd run a marathon, every inch of her aching. Sobs racked her body, and she doubled over, unable to even crawl toward the man that she loved.

She'd failed to tell him how she really felt, and now she'd lost her chance. He'd been hit, and she'd never get to tell him the truth.

Reese and whoever the third man was—maybe his partner—rushed past her, kicking Frank's gun away.

"Help him. Help him!" she screamed, pointing at Zach's splayed form. But the words didn't make it out of her mind, much less her throat. Reese seemed unconcerned. Had he not noticed?

Scrambling across the floor toward Zach, she ran her hands over his chest, searching for the blood. She could put pressure on it and save him until the ambulance arrived. Just like he'd done for her in the park.

But there was no blood. His coat was blocking it. Wrenching the pull on his zipper, she steeled herself for the crimson pool below.

Instead she found a blue vest with a smashed silver bullet right in the middle of his chest.

Her gaze shot to his face, where his beautiful brown eyes flickered open, and his mouth pulled into a tight line.

"You're not bleeding." Even she had a hard time believing the statement.

"No." He grunted, pulling at the Velcro tabs on his vest. "But it still feels like I got hit in the chest with a sledgehammer." His breathing was staggered at best, but she'd never seen anything as reassuring as the rise and fall of his chest.

She helped him slide his vest off, holding his head up until he collapsed back against the hay-covered wood. Somehow she couldn't move her hand from his shirt, checking and rechecking that he hadn't been seriously injured.

He caught her hand in his. "I'll be fine." Reaching up to run a thumb along her cheek, he said, "I'm a lot better than you, Julie."

She flinched away from his caress. Everything hurt, but she managed to smile with the side of her face that hadn't suffered a split lip. "It's Emma."

"Emma?"

"My name. I remembered."

By the time she heard the sirens, they were already upon them, swarming the yard, and paramedics pulled her away from Zach. He reached out to her, his fingers stretched long, but it didn't do any good.

Expert hands rolled him onto a yellow board, slid him onto a gurney and whisked him away.

"I'll never forget you," she whispered as they did the same to her, slamming the rear ambulance doors. Closing her eyes against the bright lights inside the bay, she succumbed to the sleep that had been calling her name.

* * *

"You have a visitor, Miss Bullock."

Emma glanced up from the magazine that the nurse had loaned to her, her heart firmly lodged in her throat. Had Zach finally come for her? It hadn't even been twenty-four hours since he'd rescued her from Frank, but each minute had felt like a lifetime.

Her parents weren't expected for a few more hours, so she let herself believe that it would be Zach, no matter how strange that he would wait to be announced instead of showing himself in. After all, he'd visited her ICU room dozens of times during her first stay in the hospital.

Could he be as nervous as she was?

"Send him in," she managed to croak.

The nurse nodded and disappeared in the direction of the waiting area.

Sitting up a little taller, Emma rearranged the skirt of her robe and pulled the lapels closer together over her hospital gown. She bunched the pillow behind her to find a more comfortable spot. Butterflies danced in her stomach, and she nibbled on her bottom lip.

What was she supposed to say to the man who had risked his life to rescue her?

Maybe he'd just kiss her, and then she wouldn't have to think of something to say.

She still wore a silly grin when her visitor arrived.

His shoes clicked on the polished floor as he strolled toward her bed, his hand outstretched. "Andre Zuri, Associated Press."

Her shoulders fell, and she sank into her pillow. A visitor. Just not the one she wanted.

She shook his hand anyway. It was clammy and limp like a fish. Definitely not the kind of shake she'd get from Zach. "Emma Bullock."

"It's very nice to meet you. I write for the Midwest bureau, and I got a tip that you've had a pretty eventful time in Minneapolis. Care to tell me about it?"

Not really.

She could come up with at least a million things she'd rather do, and at least the top one hundred involved staring at her ceiling and wondering what Zach was doing right at that minute. None of them included rehashing being stalked, attacked or kidnapped by Frank Adams and his goons.

"I heard there's a child still missing."

Her eyes opened wide. Of course. An AP article about Kay and Lonnie. Maybe it could help to locate and reunite them. If she could do nothing else, if her memories were good for nothing else, she could spread the word and pray that God brought the scared young woman and her baby back together.

It was the only thing she could do, and she had to do something.

Taking a deep breath, she offered a wavering smile. "What do you want to know? I'll tell you everything I can remember."

Zach paced the hallway at the police station, arms crossed and head bowed. He glared at the nondescript white door that led to an interrogation room. He knew that Frank Adams sat on the other side, and he ached to confront the man who had kidnapped Emma. A twinge in his right arm, where he'd slammed against the ground after being shot, was the only remaining physical evidence of their altercation, and it stung every time he thought about Adams.

But he'd promised to wait until Serena and Josh arrived. They were on their way, and a quick glance at his watch confirmed that they should arrive anytime.

The staccato click of her heels around the outskirts of the bull pen alerted him that Serena had arrived, and Josh followed right behind her. Both wore their typical attire—black suits and crisp, white shirts. Serena had done something different with her hair, twisting it up into a neat knot at the nape of her neck. And Josh, who never seemed to smile when they met, boasted a half grin.

"Good to see you both," Zach said.

"You, too." Serena ran a hand over her collar, straightening a miniscule wrinkle. "I'm sorry to hear about what happened to Emma. I wish we could have found Frank first. How is she?"

Guilt, hot and sharp, seared his midsection. He wished he'd have found Frank first, too. More than anything, he wished he had a personal report to give them. But between the cleanup at the farm, booking Adams and seeing to his own injury, Zach had had little chance to see her.

"I called the hospital this morning, and it sounds like she'll be released today. Her memory is coming back, and she was strong when I saw her last night."

"That's good news." Serena gave him a knowing smile, like she knew the truth about his feelings for Emma, but she gracefully changed the subject. "Thanks for waiting for us to talk with him."

"No problem. We have all the evidence that we need to try him for kidnapping and assault and attempted murder of a police officer, so we're happy to make sure that you get everything he can offer. I've already spoken to the assistant district attorney, and she isn't interested in a plea bargain. But the U.S. Attorney may feel differently about any federal crimes."

Josh nodded. "Let's see what Frank has to say."

Zach put his hand on the doorknob, but stopped before

opening it. "Before we go in there, what's going on with the other cases—the other missing babies?"

Crossing his arms, Josh let out a slow breath. "Have you found Kay?"

He shook his head. "No. There was no sign of her at the farm where Frank was hiding out."

"We're not much further than that with the other cases, either."

The hair on his arms stood up, a shudder running the length of his back.

Serena's mouth turned grim. "Maybe Frank will be able to give us something useful. We haven't been able to locate Don Saunders, so maybe he can shed some light on the bigger picture."

Saunders. They'd mentioned him the first time they'd come to question Julie—Emma.

Zach turned the knob in his hand.

He ushered them in before him, letting the marshals settle into seats at the table opposite Frank, whose hands were tethered with clanking chains. "Mr. Adams, I'm Detective Jones. We met last night." Adams nodded slowly, sucking on his front teeth with the tip of his tongue. "These are U.S. Marshals Summers and McCall. They'd like to ask you a few questions."

Adams's eyes, nearly black, swept over all three of them before settling back onto Zach. "And if you like what you hear?"

So the guy was ready to play the game and drop some names. Well, he could hope for a deal all he wanted. It wasn't likely to happen.

Zach shrugged. "There's little chance of that. Pretty much everything you have to say will be colored by the fact that you tried to kill a good friend of mine last night."

"You mean that…chick?"

The image of Emma at this thug's mercy buzzed through his mind, and Zach had to take three deep breaths to get his head on straight. "You know exactly who I mean." His tone was more growl than he'd expected, so he paused to clear his throat. "So start talking. No matter what, you're pretty much guaranteed convictions for assault, kidnapping of an adult and a minor—and if you took her across state lines, that's a federal crime—attempted murder and whatever else our D.A. thinks will stick. *Then* you'll face a federal court."

"You saying there's a deal in this if I talk?" Frank's eyes were filled with enough hatred to knock over a small man, but Zach pressed flat hands against the table and leaned in.

"I'm saying, we'll let you know after you tell us what happened to Kay."

"Who?"

Josh glared hard at the other man. "The missing baby. The one you stole from Emma."

"I don't know. I gave the kid to the woman just like they told me to."

Serena and Josh shared a quick glance, and Zach caught Josh's stare before he said, "We need details. What woman are you talking about?"

For the first time, Frank's shell cracked, and he gazed unblinking at his hands. "I don't know who she was. I was told to just meet her and give her the baby. That's it."

"Who told you where to meet her?" Serena's tone was even but steely.

"I don't know."

"What do you mean, you don't know? How could you not know who you were dealing with?"

With a shrug Frank sighed. "I got a phone call. They said Don—"

Josh interrupted without remorse. "Saunders?"

"Yeah. Saunders had recommended me. They said they needed a hand, and the money was good. I was just supposed to pick up some kid and deliver it to this motel. And if the mom put up a fight, I was supposed to do whatever it took."

Zach's scowl grew with each syllable. How could a man be so driven by a paycheck to steal a child and beat a woman nearly to death? "Why that baby? Why did you attack Emma?"

"They said the baby's mom was some kid who didn't want her anyway. I saw the mom give the kid to Emma, but a job's a job, right? I had my instructions, so I just did what I was supposed to."

"So why keep coming after Emma?"

Frank gave another shrug. "Loose ends. Couldn't have her identifying me, especially if I want another job. Figure there's an opening after Saunders died."

Serena's careful mask wrinkled right along with her forehead. "Don is dead?"

"Yep. Seems like someone wasn't happy with the job he was doing."

"And these are the people that you wanted to work for?" Zach couldn't keep the incredulity out of his voice.

"Hey, man, I've got certain skills." Like a heavy fist and no integrity. "I do whatever I've got to to make a living. I mean, I didn't know I was messing with a cop's girlfriend or anything, but I needed the money."

Zach's stomach twisted, but he didn't bother to correct Frank. Emma wasn't his girlfriend. But not because he didn't want her to be.

Frank kept talking—his words all following an incoherent pattern. For all his desire to broker a deal, he didn't really have much to say. They'd check out the motel where he dropped Kay off with the woman, who Frank couldn't describe and hadn't recognized.

"Hey, it was late and dark, and I was tired."

His excuses for not remembering didn't hold much weight when the reason for his exhaustion was the effort it took to attack Emma. In fact, everything he said just left a more bitter taste in Zach's mouth, and after another twenty minutes, he was more than ready to send Frank back to lockup.

As he stepped into the hallway, closing the door behind them, Zach offered his continued help to the marshals. "We'll keep looking for Kay and Lonnie and will let you know the minute that we have a new lead, but I have a feeling that Frank isn't going to be much help."

Serena pressed her hands to her hips and shook her head. "I can't believe how little he actually knew. Other than Don's death, he really gave us no new information."

"There's not a likely plea bargain in his future," Josh agreed, taking a similar stance as his partner, his hands tucked into the pockets of his pants. "But we appreciate your cooperation."

"Anytime."

Zach shook their hands and watched them walk out of the station's front door. His case was closed. Emma was safe and the right detectives were working the missing persons cases for Kay and Lonnie.

As he dropped into the chair at his desk, he stared at the blank computer screen, his mind immediately returning to the first time he'd sat in this same chair, thinking about the same girl. Then he'd thought of her as a case.

Now he knew her to be a woman who held his heart.

He'd tried to stay away. He'd tried to keep his distance, to keep from becoming too emotionally attached.

He'd failed.

Miserably.

Maybe if he just saw her one more time, that would quench the thirst to see her.

Unlikely.

But somehow it didn't stop him from calling the hospital to see if she was still there.

A soft-spoken switchboard operator answered his call.

"Yes, this is Detective Jones with the Minneapolis Police Department. Can you tell me if Emma Bullock is still checked in?"

"Well, I'll just check on that for you." The wait was nearly as awful as the news. "I'm sorry. She's checked out."

"Thank you." He settled the handset back into its cradle before scrubbing his hands over his face and shutting his eyes against the throbbing pain behind his eyes.

This is what they needed. A clean break.

Funny. It felt more like a broken heart.

SEVENTEEN

Zach still favored his right arm as he made his way across the living room to answer the doorbell. Gizmo barked at him to hurry up, wagging his tail and sniffing at the weather stripping along the threshold.

"I'm coming, boy. Hold your horses."

The eager mutt pawed at the door, bouncing with joy when Zach swung it open.

Julie—he kept forgetting that her name was Emma—stood on the porch, her hands locked in front of her. Her perfect pixie cut was styled to highlight her eyes, which were wide and as soft as melting chocolate. She bit into her bottom lip and lifted a shoulder in greeting.

He pushed the storm door open. "Come on in."

Every fiber of his being screamed that he should pull her into his arms and hold her and kiss her until they forgot everything that Frank Adams had done.

She looked just like his Julie, but she wasn't that woman anymore. There was a certainty in her eyes that had never been there before, a certainty about who she was and what she wanted.

Emma stepped into the living room, kneeling before Gizmo and scratching behind his ears. "Hey, boy. I've missed you."

Zach would have given everything he owned to hear her say that to him. Instead he fabricated a smile and responded, "He's missed you, too."

"Really?" She looked up from her position on the floor, and he crossed his arms over his chest, another barrier. Anything to keep him from reaching for her.

"I was just going to get a cup of coffee. Do you want one?"

"Sure. Thank you."

He traipsed toward the kitchen, and Gizmo's clicking nails on the hardwood floor followed right behind him. He had to keep himself from looking directly at her. If he didn't, there was no telling what he'd say or how he'd embarrass them both.

Pulling two blue mugs from the cabinet, he poured steaming liquid into them. "How are you feeling?"

When he turned, she had a hand up to her left cheek, her fingers shielding half her face. "Fine."

Which really meant that she was still covering the bruise from Adams.

He handed her a mug, and she took it, immediately pressing it against her lips. Taking a tentative sip from his own cup, he tried to come up with something to say. It hadn't been this awkward before. And he didn't have a clue what had changed.

"So where have you been staying?"

"At the Holiday Inn off the interstate. My parents are here while I give my statements, and then they're taking me back to Grand Forks."

He'd heard about her parents being in town. In fact, he'd purposely stayed away because he was sure that she'd want to spend her time with reminders of her real life and not the one that she'd fabricated with him.

Except their weeks together had sure felt real to him.

"So, you remember everything?"

She nodded slowly, never taking her eyes off her jostling coffee. "Almost. Some things are a little hazy—like everything after Frank hit me over the head until I woke up in the hospital and saw you."

Her cheeks turned a soft shade of pink, and he leaned his hip against the edge of the counter, a slow smile crossing his face. He'd remember that day for a long while, too.

"You probably saw the rest in my police statement."

"No. I haven't seen it." Actually, he didn't want to see it. When Ramirez had asked if he wanted the video of her statement, he'd turned the other detective down flat. No way was his last visual of Emma going to be an out-of-focus recording in an interrogation room. He'd gotten the highlights from the file, but the memory of her hovering over him, her hands gentle and eyes wild—that was the image he'd planned on carrying with him for the rest of his life.

This one—this twitchy, nervous version of Emma—didn't fit with that other memory.

He just had to get them to line up. "You want to tell me about it?"

From beneath long lashes, she glanced up and nodded. "I grew up in Grand Forks, North Dakota. It's a pretty big town for North Dakota, but really small compared to the Twin Cities. It's one of those places where everyone knows everyone else's business. You know?"

He smiled, hoping to keep her talking. Just the familiar sound of her voice set his heart on a faster rhythm.

"Well, I'd been dating my high school sweetheart. I thought we were going to get married. And then right before Thanksgiving last year, he told me he was in love with my best friend."

Zach grunted. That had to hurt.

She grimaced. "Yeah. It was awful, and it didn't help

that he was the quarterback of the high school football team that almost won state. Eight years later he was still revered, so everyone wanted to know what I had done to lose him. My parents were great, but they couldn't save me from all the rude questions and sideways glances. Even a couple people at church felt free to ask me probing questions to the point that I just stopped going."

He rested a hand on the counter, leaning toward her, drawn by the gentle cadence of her words. "So how did you end up in Minneapolis?"

"I'm a nurse—just like I remembered—and I worked for a pediatrician. This one day one of my old classmates brought her son in, and she thought that gave her permission to grill me about why my boyfriend had dumped me.

"And that's when I decided I needed a change of pace and a change of place. I applied for a job at the Amplatz Children's Hospital, and they asked me to come down for an interview. Mom has a tendency to worry, so in case I didn't get the job, I just told my parents I was going to visit a friend."

"Oh, I bet they were scared out of their socks when you didn't come home." Just the thought made his head spin. He'd been nearly out of his mind with worry when she'd been taken. How much worse was it for her parents when they didn't have a clue where she was or if she was in danger?

"That's putting it mildly."

"Were you just checking out the city when you met Lonnie?"

"I was leaving the hospital after my interview." Her gaze roamed the ceiling as she sought the details. "Lonnie was sitting on a bench outside, and I stopped to get a bit of fresh air. One thing led to another, and she was telling me all about her baby, and how she was afraid that Kay was in trouble." Emma's lip trembled, and she took a quick swig out of her mug to cover the tell. But she couldn't block the tears that pooled in her eyes. "Lonnie was scared. I kept telling her to take Kay to child protective services, but she was afraid of something. She just kept saying it wasn't safe and it wasn't right."

"What wasn't right?"

"I don't know."

Her gaze was lost somewhere over his shoulder, and he prodded gently. "How did you end up at McNulty's then?"

"Um…Lonnie told me that she needed to run an errand, but she couldn't take Kay with her. I should have said that I couldn't, but when she asked me to take Kay and meet her outside McNulty's near the park an hour later, I couldn't refuse."

The pain of that night was visible in the lines around her mouth as she continued. "I waited for over an hour, just like Melinda said. And I started thinking maybe I'd misunderstood. Maybe we were going to meet in the park, so I set out." She sighed loudly. "And then there were these footsteps."

"He'd been following Kay."

"I figured that." She pressed her lips into a tight line, eyes still unfocused. "He hit me so hard. It felt like my head was going to explode, but I just kept thinking that I had to protect Kay. I had to keep her safe." She didn't keep going, only hung her head low.

He stepped toward her, putting a hand under her elbow. "Hey, this isn't your fault. You did the best you could to protect her. And we're going to find her."

"I know that, but it's hard to *know*—" she thumped her chest twice "—that."

His arms itched to pull her close, to comfort her pain and remove the worry that wrinkled her forehead.

Instead he shoved his hands into his pockets.

She stared into the dregs of her mug. "I'm going back to Grand Forks this afternoon."

"That's fast." His voice cracked, and he cleared his throat, wishing it was enough to clear the pain away with it.

"Well, since Frank confessed to everything, you don't need me anymore."

That wasn't even close to the truth.

But how could he ask a woman who had known the pain of losing her family so acutely to stay? No matter how much he cared for her, it was still a selfish request. If he asked her to stay, he'd take her away from the stability she most longed for.

Dear Lord, he wanted to be selfish.

She plunked her mug down on the counter, giving him a soft smile and resting a hand on his arm. "I'm going to miss you, Zach. I can't thank you enough for everything." Her gaze seemed to bore into his chest, right at the black-and-blue bruise that still covered his sternum.

"Just doing my job." That wasn't even in the same state as the whole truth. "I'm going to miss you, too."

"Please tell Samantha, Keaton and Reese that I'm so thankful for them, too. Keep in touch. Let me know if there's anything I can do to help find Kay." Her glance swung to the door and then back again. "I wish I could stick around and help."

Strolling with her toward the front of the house, he put a hand on her shoulder. She tilted her chin up, and he couldn't help himself. He pressed a quick kiss to her cheek before pulling away and staring out the far window. That had been a very stupid idea. He couldn't go around kissing her just because he wanted to. Because now he wanted to so much more than he had before.

A soft blush pinked her cheeks, and she clasped her

hands in front her, her elbows locked at her sides. "Will you keep me updated on the case?"

"You know I can't discuss ongoing investigations, but yes. As much as I can. We won't give up until they're found. I promise."

Emma swung toward the door, then back toward him. All of the certainty that had been in her eyes was now gone. "Really. Thank you. You know, I was lost. I told myself that I wanted to leave Grand Forks because of the busybodies and rumor mill, but the truth is that I felt like God had given up on me, that He'd abandoned me. He'd taken away everything I thought I'd wanted, and I let myself pull away from Him."

She paused, and his heart stopped right along with her. He couldn't tear his gaze away from the simple beauty of her face.

"And then, when I really didn't have anything, I realized that God was still with me. I knew His words and the songs of praise that I'd been singing for years. It was like He'd written those words on the deepest part of my heart, so no matter how much I couldn't remember, I would always know the truth. God didn't abandon me. He just had something different in mind for me."

Her eyes were bright, glistening in the rays of sunlight dancing through the window, and he had no words. He longed to hear her say that she wanted to stay with him, to see what might grow between them, that God had brought them together for a reason.

When she didn't say anything, he hugged her quickly and said his goodbyes.

As he closed the door behind her, he smacked his forehead against the frame.

What kind of idiot let a girl like that go? If he thought for a second that she wanted to stay half as much as he wanted her to, then he'd have gotten on his knees and pleaded with her to never leave. But she'd said she had a life, a home to get back to. Even when she hadn't known where her home was, she'd missed it.

"Man, you're stupid."

He turned around with a start at his sister's words. "What? Why?"

"She was practically begging you to ask her to stay." Samantha pranced down the last few steps and disappeared into the kitchen.

Emma hadn't implied any such thing.

Had she?

Emma trotted down the steps in her parents' modest Grand Forks home. She'd grown up here, and most of the pictures on the wall and nearly all the stories they told were connected to an actual memory from her childhood. The curtain had been pulled back until there were only a few dark spots in the recesses of her mind.

Her parents had insisted that she stay with them for a couple weeks, and she'd been glad not to be alone in her apartment—not because she was afraid. Frank was locked up and she was safe.

But just like it had at the hospital that first night after the showdown on the farm, a bittersweetness threatened to choke her. She had so much to be thankful for, yet knowing that she'd likely never see Zach again made her hands shake and her lungs burn.

Her cell phone rang. Another unfamiliar number with a Minneapolis area code. It was probably the hospital again. They'd offered her the job at the children's hospital—the one she'd interviewed for right before meeting Lonnie. And the head of nursing was eager for her response.

She stared at the bright screen but let it go to voice mail. Their third call that week.

The job was really everything she'd hoped for. But could she be so close to Zach and not speak with him? Or worse, could she push down her feelings and just be his friend?

Grand Forks was safe. It was familiar. And she wasn't alone.

But it didn't have Zach.

As she fell onto the couch in the living room, the landline rang. That would be another reporter looking for her story, digging for something more than the AP article that had run online and in newspapers across the country. She'd had about a dozen calls from them, and still she didn't want to talk about it again.

Closing her eyes against the strength of the sun that made the living room curtains seem feeble, she prayed for peace. She needed to make a decision.

"God, I could use a sign here."

Nothing happened. No clear sign or writing on the wall.

She hadn't expected that. But a strong feeling in her stomach would have helped. No clear answer presented itself, but a gentle peace rolled over her, swallowing her like a favorite blanket on a winter night.

Before the attack, before her time in Minneapolis, God had felt so distant, like a dream that she couldn't quite remember in the midst of the heartache of being dumped and publicly humiliated. In the middle of her amnesia, unable to remember the pain of a broken heart, she'd remembered the truth, what it was like to know God was close, to speak to Him like a friend, to call on Him in her hour of need.

Despite the pain, God had not abandoned her. And He would see her through the difficult days to come, too.

When the doorbell chimed, she pushed herself up to peek out the window. The figure on the front step faced away from her, his head hung low and his hands shoved into the pockets of his jeans.

Before she consciously recognized the slope of his broad shoulders, her heart began an erratic dance, alternately fluttering and pounding as she scrambled for the door. It took a lifetime to get over the back of the couch and across the entryway, and by the time she swung the door open, she was panting and dizzy.

But there he stood, the man she'd been dreaming about. "Zach."

It was more breath than spoken word, but he turned his head just the same. A gentle smile crept across his mouth, and he pressed a hand to his chest like his heart was suffering the same sweet torture as her own.

"Hi, Emma."

"Hi." Could she sound any more vapid? But other words refused to surface, so she let her body take over, throwing her arms around his neck and hugging him with all of the pent-up emotions of the past three weeks.

His arms wrapped around her waist, and he whispered into her hair. "I tried to call."

"I haven't been answering the phone. Haven't wanted to talk to anyone." Letting go only enough to look into his face, she smiled. "Until now."

His grin spread, but when he released her, she was forced to do the same. "Are your parents around? I'd like to meet them."

"No. They're both at work, but they'll be back tonight." She waved him toward the living room. "Come in. Tell me what you're doing here."

He stepped into the foyer, but stopped on the tile entry, his hands going back into his pockets, his forehead tense. He looked as unsure as a kid on his first day of school.

Crossing her arms, she waited, watched. The strong line

of his jaw worked back and forth, his nose twitching in the silence. This wasn't good news. "Is it Frank? Did he escape or did the judge let him go?"

"Frank?" He looked utterly confused. "No. Nothing like that."

"Then—please don't get me wrong, I'm happy to see you—but what are you doing here?"

The tiny dimple in his right cheek made its first appearance of the day. Throwing up his hands, he said, "I couldn't stay away."

Her stomach did a full flip. She couldn't have heard him right, could she? He didn't mean what she thought he meant, did he?

With outstretched hands, he took three steps toward her until he could twine their fingers together. "I let you go because I thought it was what you wanted. You talked about how much you missed your family, and I couldn't ask you to stay, but I never wanted you to go."

"Why no-ot?" Her voice cracked, her mouth suddenly bone-dry.

A muscle in his jaw jumped. "Because I am so in love with you."

The back of her eyes burned, and she blinked hard against the rush of tears. It was everything she'd longed for. Everything.

And yet a voice in the back of her mind that sounded an awful lot like Samantha reminded her that he liked to take in strays. He'd been caring for lost animals for years, and he'd admitted that it was hard to give them up when the time came. Was she really so different from them?

His outline turned fuzzy, and she broke his hold to brush away the moisture in her eyes.

"Hey." His thumb captured a tear that had escaped and headed toward her chin. "Tell me what you're thinking."

"I'm not a stray."

"I don't understand." His brows wrinkled like he was trying hard to.

"You took in Gizmo and other animals and you care for them. And that's part of who you are, and I love that about you. But I don't want to be another stray."

His fingers combed her hair over her ear and then cupped her head as his dimple returned. "A stray? Not even close."

"No?"

"Sweet Emma, I have fallen so hard for you. When your memories were gone, I got to see your true heart." He shook his head as if he still couldn't believe it, and her true heart pounded with joy. "You are filled with compassion and determination, and you're full of pluck and smarts, and I've been a complete fool. I never should have let you leave Minneapolis without telling you the truth."

"Really?"

"It's no easy task loving a homicide detective, and I thought you'd be better off without me. I thought it would be best to give you up, to let you go back to your family. I was wrong." The intensity of his tone sent tremors through her hands, and he glanced at the one he still held in his own. "Are you afraid? Did I scare you?"

Words failed her, so she just shook her head, stepping into the circle of his arms. He smelled clean and earthy, like fresh rain. Resting her hands on his chest, she could feel his short gasp and the tempo of his heart as it sailed. Her breath caught as his smile turned saucy, his arms tightening around her back.

"So, what do you say?" She still couldn't see anything above his lips as they formed his question.

"About?" she asked.

"Well, I just told you that I'm in love with you. Do you have anything to say about that?"

"I'm so glad."

He laughed, and she couldn't wait a second more. Pushing onto her tiptoes and pulling herself up on his shoulders, she pressed her lips to his. Fire and pleasure shot through her, making every inch of her skin tingle with delight.

She was safe. She was treasured. She was loved.

All the fear and uncertainty was behind them; this was the future she wanted.

When he finally pulled away, his eyes sparkled. "I'll take that to mean you love me, too."

"I do. I so very much do."

He kissed her again, sweet and powerful. "I guess this means I'd better move to Grand Forks."

"And quit the force?"

A shadow of sorrow crossed his face for a split second, replaced with a smile almost as quickly as it had appeared. "It'll be worth it to be near you."

He'd never sacrifice a career he loved for a stray. Actually, he'd never have risked his life for a stray. Why hadn't she seen it that night on the farm? She thought he'd just been doing his job, but the truth was he'd risked everything to save her life. He'd been willing to lay down his own life for hers. And there was no greater love than that.

That sure knowledge warmed her chest until laughter bubbled forth. "Oh, please don't quit your job. It's so much a part of who you are, of the man I'm in love with."

His face puckered as if he'd sucked on a lemon. "I don't want to be that far away from you."

"Then I'll move to Minneapolis. The children's hospital called and offered me the job I interviewed for. I think I'll take it."

Without warning he hauled her back to his chest and kissed her soundly. Pressing his forehead to hers, he took a ragged breath. "We're going to have a good life together, Emma."

"I know."

Although not quite all of her memories had returned, she was certain that at Zach's side, the best were yet to be made.

* * * * *

Dear Reader,

I'm so glad that you joined Zach, Julie and me in this exciting installment of the Witness Protection series.

Writing about Julie's amnesia was so much fun for me. I had to ask myself time and again what was so ingrained in her character that no amount of forgotten memories could steal it away. I was reminded of a promise in Hebrews that God will put His laws on our hearts and write His words in our minds. No matter how distant she felt from God, His promises were true.

I hope you'll remember that, during times when God feels far away.

Thanks for spending your time with us. I appreciate it more than I can express. And I'd love to hear from you. You can reach me at liz@lizjohnsonbooks.com, Twitter.com/LizJohnsonBooks or Facebook.com/LizJohnsonBooks.

I've loved working with the other talented authors in this miniseries to give you a thrilling tale. Be sure to pick up the future books in the series coming in April, May and June.

Liz Johnson

Questions for Discussion

1. Which character in this book do you most relate to? What makes you say that?

2. From the first chapter Julie deals with amnesia. What would be the scariest part about having amnesia for you personally?

3. There are some things that Julie believes she would never forget—like if she were married. What's something that you're certain you wouldn't forget even if you lost every other memory?

4. Julie remembers all the words to "It is Well with My Soul." Is there a hymn that you think is so ingrained in your heart that you'd never forget it? What makes that song meaningful to you?

5. Zach describes several characteristics that are at the very heart of Julie, that her amnesia can't touch. What are a few traits that you believe you'd always carry?

6. Can you identify with the inadequacies that Julie feels that make her compare herself to a stray? Why or why not?

7. Much of Zach and Julie's story is about waiting for God's timing. As hard as they try to unlock Julie's memories, it only happens in the right time. Have you had a similar experience where you tried to rush something that you couldn't control?

8. One of Zach's best friends is LeRoy, a reformed drug dealer who runs a rehabilitation center. What do you think that friendship says about Zach's heart?

9. How do you think Zach's history with friends like LeRoy helped him feel comfortable falling in love with a woman without any memories?

10. Do you think that you could ever fall in love with someone without knowing his or her past? Why?

11. Why do you think Zach and Julie are a good match for each other?

12. Do you think that the marshals will find baby Kay and reunite her with her mom, Lonnie?

REQUEST YOUR FREE BOOKS!

2 FREE RIVETING INSPIRATIONAL NOVELS
PLUS 2 FREE MYSTERY GIFTS

Love Inspired®
SUSPENSE

YES! Please send me 2 FREE Love Inspired® Suspense novels and my 2 FREE mystery gifts (gifts are worth about $10). After receiving them, if I don't wish to receive any more books, I can return the shipping statement marked "cancel." If I don't cancel, I will receive 4 brand-new novels every month and be billed just $4.74 per book in the U.S. or $5.24 per book in Canada. That's a savings of at least 21% off the cover price. It's quite a bargain! Shipping and handling is just 50¢ per book in the U.S. and 75¢ per book in Canada.* I understand that accepting the 2 free books and gifts places me under no obligation to buy anything. I can always return a shipment and cancel at any time. Even if I never buy another book, the two free books and gifts are mine to keep forever.

123/323 IDN F5AC

Name _____ (PLEASE PRINT) _____

Address _____ Apt. # _____

City _____ State/Prov. _____ Zip/Postal Code _____

Signature (if under 18, a parent or guardian must sign)

Mail to the Harlequin® Reader Service:
IN U.S.A.: P.O. Box 1867, Buffalo, NY 14240-1867
IN CANADA: P.O. Box 609, Fort Erie, Ontario L2A 5X3

**Are you a current subscriber to Love Inspired Suspense books
and want to receive the larger-print edition?
Call 1-800-873-8635 or visit www.ReaderService.com.**

* Terms and prices subject to change without notice. Prices do not include applicable taxes. Sales tax applicable in N.Y. Canadian residents will be charged applicable taxes. Offer not valid in Quebec. This offer is limited to one order per household. Not valid for current subscribers to Love Inspired Suspense books. All orders subject to credit approval. Credit or debit balances in a customer's account(s) may be offset by any other outstanding balance owed by or to the customer. Please allow 4 to 6 weeks for delivery. Offer available while quantities last.

Your Privacy—The Harlequin® Reader Service is committed to protecting your privacy. Our Privacy Policy is available online at www.ReaderService.com or upon request from the Harlequin Reader Service.
We make a portion of our mailing list available to reputable third parties that offer products we believe may interest you. If you prefer that we not exchange your name with third parties, or if you wish to clarify or modify your communication preferences, please visit us at www.ReaderService.com/consumerschoice or write to us at Harlequin Reader Service Preference Service, P.O. Box 9062, Buffalo, NY 14269. Include your complete name and address.

LIS13R

SPECIAL EXCERPT FROM

Love Inspired®
SUSPENSE

Morgan Smith is hiding in the Witness Protection
Program. Has her past come back to haunt her?

Read on for a preview of
TOP SECRET IDENTITY by Sharon Dunn,
the next exciting book in the
WITNESS PROTECTION series
from Love Inspired Suspense. Available April 2014.

A wave of terror washed over Morgan Smith when she
heard the tapping at her window. Someone was outside the
caretaker's cottage. Had the man who'd tried to kill her in
Mexico found her in Iowa?

Though she'd been in witness protection for two months,
her fear of being killed had never subsided. She'd left
Des Moines for the countryside and a job at a stable because she had felt exposed in the city, vulnerable. She'd
grown up on a ranch in Wyoming, and when she'd worked
as an American missionary in Mexico, she'd always chosen
to be in rural areas. Wide-open spaces seemed safer to her.

With her heart pounding, she rose to her feet and walked
the short distance to the window, half expecting to see a face
contorted with rage, or clawlike hands reaching for her neck.
The memory of nearly being strangled made her shudder.
She stepped closer to the window, seeing only blackness. Yet
the sound of the tapping had been too distinct to dismiss as
the wind rattling the glass.

A chill snaked down her spine.

Someone was outside.

If the man from Mexico had come to kill her, it seemed odd that he would give her a warning by tapping on the window.

She thought to call her new boss, who was in the guesthouse less than a hundred yards away. Alex Reardon seemed like a nice man. She'd hated being evasive when he'd asked her where she had gotten her knowledge of horses. She'd been blessed to get the job without references. Her references, everything and everyone she knew, all of that had been stripped from her, even her name. She was no longer Magdalena Chavez. Her new name was Morgan Smith.

The knob on the locked door turned and rattled.

She'd been a fool to think the U.S. Marshals could keep her safe.

Pick up TOP SECRET IDENTITY wherever
Love Inspired® Suspense books and ebooks are sold.

LISEXP0314